Land of Nod
The Artifact

Gary Hoover

Edited by Christy Rabe

And

Danielle Raver

Cover Art by:

David Ellis

http://dbellis.daportfolio.com/

Title and Lay-Out by:

Ceri Clark

Find out more about future books at:

http://www.landofnodtrilogy.com

And

http://www.facebook.com/landofnodtrilogy

Two Men Say They're Jesus
One of Them Must be Wrong

-Mark Knopfler

Chapter 1:

The boredom was almost painful.

Jeff aimed the remote.

Up, up, up...

He didn't pause long enough on any channel to really see what was happening. He knew there was nothing worth watching. There was *NEVER* anything worth watching. Jeff was like a chimpanzee pulling the hairs out of his arm... one... by... one.

Who was it who said: 'Insanity is doing the same thing over and over again and expecting different results'? Jeff wondered to himself. *Einstein? Yeah, like he was one to judge sanity.*

"Faced with evidence that either he was crazy or the universe was crazy," Jeff's father had told him, "Einstein decided: *'It must be the universe.'* And damned if he wasn't right."

Jeff laughed, then shook his head to try to rattle some of the crazy out of it.

It didn't work.

Could boredom actually lead to madness? Was it possible for one's brain to become so disinterested with the mundanity of life that it started dreaming while the person was still awake?

Up, up, up...

His mom had given up on trying to force him to go to bed at a decent hour. Jeff was deft at playing the 'I still haven't gotten over the loss of my father' card.

He felt like he had to do something, anything, other than what he was doing.

Drifting.

Up, up, up...

It was the kind of boredom that made Jeff's brain itchy.

Beneath the skull where it was hard to scratch.

Not that he hadn't tried.

Somehow he felt that if he stayed up long enough, the next day wouldn't come, but it always did. And it was always worse when he hadn't gotten enough sleep.

And then there were the dreams.

For the last several months, Jeff had been having *terrible* dreams.

Dreams of a savage creature – somewhat human, but reptilian. It had a powerful, sinewy body. It had jagged, uneven teeth, but it wasn't the obvious physical power and danger that got to Jeff. There was something else that burrowed into Jeff's soul like a parasitic worm making its way through the flesh to the vital bits.

Something in the eyes.

Evil, red glowing eyes that ate into him.

He'd try to get away, but his limbs wouldn't respond.

Push... move... run... scream...

Then nothing but the sound of his breathing and the darkness of his bedroom.

By the light of day, it all seemed so silly.

Monsters?

Jeff was fourteen – too old to be afraid of monsters.

It all seemed easy enough to brush off when he was awake, but when he was asleep, it had almost...

A *power* over him.

Jeff seemed to shift between three different moods, none of them good. Boredom shifted to fear. Fear shifted to sadness.

Jeff paused on a 'news' channel. Jeff was too young to remember when television actually broadcast news.

This was really a 'Republicans and Democrats arguing with a healthy dose of celebrity gossip thrown in between' channel, but as far as Jeff knew it was 'news'.

A Republican congressman had just been caught in an affair, so of course, the left-wing nut was horrified while the right-wing nut thought it was no big deal. Sometime in the near future – maybe a week, maybe a month – a Democratic congressman would be caught in an affair and their roles would switch.

Jeff decided that, if his goal was to fend off madness, his tactic wasn't working.

He rubbed his eyes, twisted in his seat and squinted – trying to bring the clock on the wall into focus.

Damn!

He pushed down on the arms of his chair and...

Nothing happened.

He tried again, using far more effort than someone as young and healthy as he was should have needed. He managed to heft himself and started the long walk to bed.

Chapter 2:

Jeff pulled the door shut behind him and looked up the street. The sun hadn't come up yet, and that wasn't helping him put the dream behind him. He knew the whole thing was silly, but he needed the bright light of day for his rational and irrational sides to come to agreement on that point.

The wind stung his neck. He pulled on the zipper of his jacket but found it was already as high as it would go.

There was an eerie, uncomfortable quiet. Jeff stood there for a moment, exhaled loudly, watched his breath swirl and disperse then headed toward the bus stop.

As he walked, he heard nothing but the sound of his own feet.

It almost seemed that he was the only thing that was real.

He looked down and watched his own feet lift, glide, fall. He had seen the other students gathered at the bus stop ahead, but – for just a few more moments – he imagined there was no one but him.

"Hey, Jeff!"

Jeff smiled. "Hey, Larry." He paused. As he snapped back to reality, he remembered that he hadn't completed the algebra assignment. "Hey, did you get that assignment for Martelli's class?"

Jeff used to be a great student, but ever since he lost his father, he couldn't seem to concentrate on anything. He always felt off balance and out of place. It seemed like he should be doing *something*.

But he had no idea what that 'something' was.

"Yeah, it wasn't too bad. You just have to get the variables on one side." Larry could see the incomprehension on Jeff's face. "Here, I'll show you." He opened the book and began to explain.

"Yo, dweebo."

Jeff and Larry both cringed. It was Jake – a monster of a ninth grader. At 6'1" and 220 lbs, he would be big for an adult, but he was huge for a fourteen year old. And to make matters worse, he was an absolute ass.

Jeff had once walked into the boy's room to find Jake peeing on the floor and laughing as if it was the funniest, most clever thing he had seen since the last Jackass movie.

Jake snatched Larry's book and tossed it to his friend, Todd. Todd wasn't much bigger than the other ninth graders, but he didn't need to be. As long as he hung around Jake, nobody would ever give him any trouble.

Larry reached for the book, but Todd tossed it to Jake who had moved a little farther away. Larry shifted directions, headed back toward Jake, and Jake tossed it back to Todd.

Jeff felt like he should do something.

He felt like it was his fault.

Jeff got along with most people and was usually not the target of bullies.

He sort of liked it that way.

He wasn't sure how far that neutral status would take him in this situation, but he had to try. "Jake, come on."

Jake seemed a little surprised that anyone would have the nerve to do anything other than just stand there uncomfortably. "Jake, come *ooooon*," he said mockingly and then held out his hands for Todd to toss the book back.

Jeff felt an uncomfortable twinge in his stomach and a tingling in his arms and legs. As Todd tossed the book, Jeff tried to intercept, but as he leaned in, Jake shoved him angrily. Jeff flailed back awkwardly and off balance as the book hit the ground with a loud 'thwap'.

That flipped a switch in Jake's brain.

He turned toward Jeff, reached out and grabbed two handfuls of Jeff's jacket. Jeff reacted instinctively and punched him as hard as he was able in the stomach. Jake let go of the jacket and stared dumbly for a moment.

Did I actually hurt him? Jeff wondered to himself. Before he could think much more, Jake exploded in a rage. He grabbed Jeff's jacket again, lifted him a couple inches off the ground and then slammed him hard onto his back. Jeff felt his teeth rattle, and pain shot through his kidneys as he hit the frozen lawn.

Jake punched wildly at him. Jeff looped one arm over his face and another around his chest in an attempt to shield himself. Most of the blows hit him on his ribs and arms. They hurt but didn't do any real damage.

"Jake! Bus is coming," Todd yelled.

The pounding stopped.

Jeff felt dizzy and lightheaded.

Everything went silent and blank for a moment, and then Jeff began to see clouds drift in and out of focus.

As he regained more of his senses, he could see shadows moving around him as the other students lined up for the bus.

Jeff felt an arm grab his, and the next thing he knew, he was standing.

"Thanks," he mumbled to Larry who looked more shaken than Jeff felt.

They got on the bus, and Jeff dropped into a seat. He avoided looking directly at Jake, but he didn't need to see him to know the Neanderthal was mouthing threats.

"After school, you're dead, Browning."

Chapter 3:

Oh hell, Jeff thought to himself as he found it even harder than usual to concentrate in history.

He tapped the eraser from his nearly new pencil on his desk – trying to see how many times he could get it to bounce. Jeff wondered if he could get away with a quick trip to the pencil sharpener. He took as many chances as he could get to stretch his legs and look out the window. *By the end of the day, this nice new pencil will be nothing but a nub,* he thought.

By the end of the day...

Jeff considered 'missing' the bus. It was about a three mile walk. Jeff could handle it, but...

No. That would be a cowardly move.

Jeff wondered what his father would have said about the situation with Jake.

Jeff couldn't imagine his father ever being afraid of anything. He wasn't physically strong, but mentally...

Dr. Browning was the sort of person who felt there wasn't anything he couldn't do, and that confidence was always visible. Jeff's father projected the ability to do anything well. If, for example, he was picking up dog poop in a plastic bag, someone would likely say: *'Wow! That guy really knows how to pick up dog poop in a plastic bag.'*

Jeff remembered that his father had talked to him once about fighting: "For all the *potential* fights people get into, there are very few actual fights. Both parties know how the fight's going to go before it happens, so the guy who knows he's going to get beat backs down before things get ugly." And Jeff had seen that scenario play out several times since his father shared that little bit of wisdom.

Problem was, he knew the outcome of his fight with Jake, and it didn't end with Jeff still standing.

His only hope in a fight with Jake would be that one of Jake's arms might, by chance, fall off during the fight.

That wasn't likely to happen.

And, truth be told, Jake could probably still kick Jeff's ass with only one arm.

"What are your thoughts, Jeff?"

Caught!

Jeff realized he had no idea what Mr. Murphy was talking about. Jeff normally enjoyed Mr. Murphy's class and respected him, so he was particularly embarrassed.

"Uhhhh..." He hoped for some hint.

"What would the punishment have been?"

"Uhhh..."

"For those who signed the Declaration of Independence?"

"Death?"

"Yes!"

Mr. Murphy clapped his hands shuffled his feet in what appeared to Jeff to be a piss-poorly executed dance step of some sort.

Nothing like the thought of someone else's pain and death to get a ninth grade teacher all giddy. I guess if they didn't enjoy suffering, they wouldn't stay ninth grade teachers for long.

With that out of the way, Jeff was once again free to imagine various scenarios for what would happen when the final bell rang.

They all ended with one of two possible outcomes: Jeff, invariably, wound up either badly beaten or a coward – afraid to ever show his face in school again.

The more Jeff thought of it, the more he decided he liked the idea of getting his ass kicked best. It would only hurt for a little bit, and then it would be over.

Jake wouldn't hurt him... much. Even Jake – who thought WWF wrestling was real, and *Jackass* was the best movie ever made – was too smart for that. Jake wouldn't want to end up in juvenile detention or facing a lawsuit for maiming a fatherless boy. No, he'd beat him – soundly –

and that would be the end of it. Maybe Jake would even end up with some respect for Jeff if he had the balls to not run from a sure thrashing.

Yep. That's it. Stand up. Take it like a man. Show up the next day beaten but not a coward.

Once he made that decision, he felt so relieved he was practically ecstatic. He glided to his locker after final period.

It was the oddest thing.

He was roughly fifteen minutes away from a good beating, yet he felt more *alive* than he had in over a year.

Chapter 4:

Jeff boarded the bus proudly. *That's right, I'm here... surprised?* He thought to himself.

He looked back at Jake who was in the back of the bus. Jeff didn't stare, but he made sure not to avoid him either. He saw Todd point at him and laugh along with Jake.

When they arrived at their stop, Jeff got up and made his way, calmly, to the door. He could feel Jake breathing down the back of his neck, and he could hear him mumbling in a mocking voice: "Jeffrey... Jeffrey"

Jeff hopped out of the bus. He didn't turn around, but he didn't run either. He was there, available for the worst Jake had to offer as soon as the bus pulled away.

Jeff watched the bus pull out of sight, and then – just so it was clear he wasn't about to run – he stopped and turned around.

And then...

One of the strangest things happened.

Nothing.

Jake was walking the other way, talking to Todd. For a brief second, Jake glanced over his shoulder at Jeff but then quickly snapped his head back around.

Jeff was almost disappointed.

Chapter 5:

I am your God.
Jeff's foot hovered over an ant.
I have the power of life or death over you. One simple move of my foot and you will cease to exist.

Jeff leaned back and stretched. He closed his eyes and felt the warmth of the sun on his face as he reclined on the steps leading to his front porch.

As often happened, his thoughts drifted to his father.

Jeff's father, Dr. Jeffrey Browning, was a brilliant physicist who had contributed significantly to the models of super-string theory. Dr. Browning was absolutely convinced that a unifying theory was within reach, but his last paper sat locked in a roll top desk gathering dust just seven feet above where Jeff Jr. spent his evenings catatonically flipping through channels.

It had been over a year ago. Jeff came home from baseball practice, pushed open the front door he had an immediate sense that something just wasn't right.

Jeff's mom, Marie, was upset. It was 7:00 PM and Jeff Senior hadn't come home yet. Not particularly unusual, unless you knew Dr. Browning. He was always *exactly* where he was supposed to be — reliable without fail. He didn't just wander off places. He had left his lab at 3:00 PM and told a late-working grad student that he was headed home.

Marie got home at 5:00 expecting her husband to be home — as he always was when he said he would be.

After a number of phone calls that confirmed he had, indeed, left for home several hours earlier, Marie knew something was wrong.

She called the police, but they told her he was probably out for a beer with some friends and would return shortly. They told her to call again the next day if, by chance, he didn't show up later that evening.

He never did show up.

Not the next hour, not the next day, not the next week.

The media latched onto the story and set up camp for a few weeks. Meanwhile, the police did their best. Nearly everyone agreed that Dr. Browning simply wasn't the sort of person who would just run away without a word. The police felt sure there was foul play of some sort, but they didn't have any clues.

It seemed he had just vanished.

The last person to see him was a grad student. "We were getting good results, and he was looking forward to the next readings. He was in a great mood, and he seemed his normal self that afternoon," the grad-student had told police.

He had walked to work, so there was no car to offer clues.

The police were absolutely baffled.

Dr. Browning was a good-natured man who had no enemies. He was financially comfortable but by no means rich enough to attract kidnappers. It was broad daylight, and nobody in the area reported any unusual activity of any kind. He was a responsible, loving husband and father who didn't have any debts, girlfriends or anything else that might entice him to run away.

The best guess investigators could offer was that he was a victim of a random crime that got out of hand, and his attacker had successfully hidden the body without leaving any traces.

Jeff stretched against the stairs. He tried to focus on the feeling of the sun on his skin.

Even after a year and several months, there was still a feeling of uncertain confusion. Jeff and his mother kept hoping Jeffrey Sr. would walk through the door any minute, but both of them seemed to know, somewhere deep in their subconscious, he would never come back.

Since they had to at least pretend there was hope – even when hope began to seem irrational – they never got the chance to really be sad or angry.

Jeff looked up and down the street – almost feeling that if he looked hard enough he'd see his father walking home.

It felt like there was something he should do.

It was almost as if he could have an answer if he thought hard enough. Jeff always thought that of his father. He felt Dr. Browning could figure anything out if he just thought about it hard enough.

Jeff felt like there was something...

A force pulling him.

He shook his head to clear his mind.

A different ant was making its way toward Jeff's sneaker. Its antennae twisted and twitched as it meandered – seemingly aimlessly but never stopping. Something kept it going.

Jeff wondered if it had any concept of what was going on around it. *Does it have any sort of primitive understanding at all or is it simply being driven by chemical signals? Do I have any understanding or am I just using a different form of those primitive signals?*

Jeff shifted the position of his sneaker and held it over the ant. The ant seemed to pause. *Does it know that its life is in my hands? Does it know that with one, small move I can crush it... for no better reason than for my own amusement?*

Jeff mentally commanded the ant to stop.

It didn't.

Jeff mentally commanded it to turn left.

It didn't.

And as the ant wandered, so did Jeff's mind.

He thought back to a time when he was seven or eight. He and his father were walking through a flea market, and Jeff spotted a set of matching lockets. He thought they were the coolest things: "Can we get them Daddy?"

His father seemed reluctant at first – likely thinking it was a waste and just two more things to clutter drawers – but he softened when he looked into his son's eyes.

When they got home, they cut two small photos: One of Jeff Junior for Jeff Senior's locket and vice versa.

For a year, they each wore their lockets day and night, but one day Jeff Jr. decided he was too old for something so silly. He took it off and left it on his dresser.

A few days later, Dr. Browning noticed Jeff wasn't wearing it. "Where's your locket?" he asked pulling his own out of his shirt by the chain and opening it.

"Ummmm, I'm not a little kid anymore, you know, Dad."

His father smiled as he admired the photo in his with a father's pride. "Well... If you don't mind... I think I might keep wearing mine. I've become sort of... attached ... to it."

"Sure, I don't care." Jeff shrugged.

"Do you think I could have yours – to keep safe in case you ever want it later?" his father asked.

"Sure." Jeff ran to his room and found the locket on the corner of his dresser where he left it. He ran back to his father's office.

His father extended an open hand. He had huge hands with long, spindly fingers. He had been quite a piano player when he was younger.

Jeff dropped the locket and watched his father's long fingers close. They both looked at the hand for a few moments. Jeff felt embarrassed. His father seemed a little sad but also proud that Jeff wasn't a 'little kid anymore'.

Dr. Browning opened a desk drawer and dropped the locket. "I'll just leave it right here in case you ever change your mind."

Jeff's upper lip trembled a bit as he thought back to that moment about four years ago. The locket suddenly seemed to mean so much more than it had back then. Back then, it was just a stupid toy he had outgrown. But at that moment it was all he had left of his father.

But do I even have it?

He assumed it was still in the drawer, *or did Dad move it?*

Jeff panicked for a moment realizing the locket might very well be just as lost as his father. At that moment, it felt so important that he wondered why he hadn't thought of it before.

The locket seemed like the most important thing in the world.

Chapter 6:

"Don't bother your father while he's working," his mother would warn sternly whenever she caught Jeff in Dr. Browning's office.

The office was an amazing place to a little kid. It was filled with electronic gadgets – radio parts, lasers, computers.

Some of the gadgets were related to Dr. Browning's work, but most of them were just toys or junk that he found interesting. He could always justify playing with toys – plasma balls, parabolic mirrors etc. – by telling himself and others that they sparked his mind. He often came up with his most creative ideas by playing with a diverse range of toys that helped him get past road-blocks in his thought.

"Necessity may be the mother of invention, but doing something because it might be cool is the weird, drunken uncle of invention. Sometimes weird, drunken uncles will teach you things your mother won't," Jeff's father once told him with a wink.

Dr. Browning never seemed to mind when Jeff bothered him while he was 'working', but he was always very specific in his warnings that Jeff should NEVER go in there alone.

Some of the devices were delicate.

Some were even dangerous.

Jeff's father also had rivals who wouldn't mind getting a peek at his notes and experiments, so he generally kept the office locked when he wasn't there.

Jeff tried the door just to see.

Locked.

It had been open when the police had been there, so Jeff thought there was a chance his mother had left it unlocked. That detail had been one of the things that had puzzled the police. The office had been unlocked, and the keys were on the desk.

They thought that might have been a clue, but even that little bit of information, while interesting, didn't seem to get them anywhere. His wallet was gone, and the police theorized that he had stopped home before going back out for something.

Jeff headed to his parent's room.

His mother had kept things as they had been, and Dr. Browning's dresser still had photos of Jeff and his mother. Back behind the photos, there was a small wooden box where Dr. Browning kept his loose change, keys and other odds and ends. Jeff hoped his mom had put the keys back there after the police had left.

Apparently she had.

Jeff grabbed a set of keys that were clearly labeled: "University – Lab", "University – Classroom", "Home – Front Door", "University – Office" and the one Jeff was looking for, "Home – Lab/Office".

Jeff smiled to himself. His father always seemed to be organized far beyond what most people would consider practical.

Jeff went back to the office and inserted the key.

It didn't seem quite right. Jeff jiggled it and tried a few times then looked at the label – "Home – Lab/Office" *That should be right*, but it clearly wasn't working.

He went back to the box on his father's dresser and checked for any loose keys.

Nope.

Jeff tried to think like his father. Dr. Browning was very bright, very organized and very efficient.

He'd want the key to be easy to get when he needed it. He wouldn't want to have to come all the way back to his room just because he forgot to get the key. He'd probably keep it somewhere close to the office... but where? He wouldn't want it to be too obvious, otherwise what would be the point of locking it at all?

Jeff looked for hiding places near the office door. He

moved a few plants, felt around the door frame but couldn't find anything.

He stood there stumped. *Think, think, think like Dad.* He looked around and tried to imagine he was his father. *He'd want it convenient but not too convenient. Maybe a little farther away.*

Jeff went down the hall checking behind some picture frames. He tried to think about times he had seen his father open the office, but he had never seen him getting keys out of hiding places.

His mother would know where it was. She had locked it after the police were there. *Did she put it somewhere else? Damn it! It can't be that hard.*

Why would he even change the lock in the first place? After he changed the lock, why would he keep the old key?

Wait a minute.

Jeff pulled the keys back out of his pocket.

He tried the "University – Classroom" key. *Nope.* The "Home - Front Door" didn't seem to work either.

Then he tried the "University – Office"

And...

It worked!

Genius!

Jeff smiled as he considered his father's thought process. He didn't need to label the keys accurately. He could easily remember that "University – Office" unlocked his home office, but if someone who was up to no good got his keys, he, like Jeff, would try the one labeled "Home – Lab/Office", and when that didn't work, he'd go looking elsewhere – just like Jeff had done, never realizing that he had the correct key in his hand.

If Dr. Browning had labeled them: "A, B, C..." or simply left them un-labeled, someone would try all of them until he found the right one.

Brilliant.

Chapter 7:

Jeff flicked the light-switch and headed for the desk. He pulled the bottom desk drawer and found the locket exactly where he had seen his father put it those many years ago.

Yes! Jeff felt a warmth wash over him as he put the chain over his head and dropped the locket into his shirt. He knew it was just his imagination, but the warmth almost felt like a real, physical sensation.

But as the initial relief and feeling of 'rightness' began to fade, he began to get uncomfortable. This was the first time he had ever been in the office alone. He felt like he shouldn't be there. It felt wrong, but his curiosity was getting the better of him.

There was a quarter 'floating' over a parabolic mirror. Jeff knew it was an illusion and not actually there, but he reached for it anyway. He smiled as his finger slipped through the image. It brought back memories of being in the office with his father. He felt like his father was a magician back then. There seemed nothing he couldn't do.

Beside the parabolic mirror was an odd electronic device that looked like a large, metal doughnut covered with electronic components. It had wires and conduits that were plugged into some sort of power source/controller several feet away.

Jeff poked his finger into the opening in the toroid but then quickly withdrew it and jumped back as the device whirred to life.

That's cool, he thought as the initial surprise wore off. There was a ring of blue lights around the top edge of the toroid, and the unit was emitting a low-frequency, fluctuating hum.

Jeff slowly edged his hand back toward the opening.

I'm an idiot, he confessed to himself but didn't back off. He put his fingers into the opening. He half expected to feel an electric shock, but didn't feel anything.

And that was the really strange part.

He didn't feel *anything*.

His fingers should have hit the table surface, but there seemed to be a hole cut in the table – which wouldn't have been too unusual except that Jeff could swear he had seen the table surface through the toroid before it had whirred to life.

Without withdrawing his hand, he leaned down and looked at the underside of the table. It seemed completely intact. He knocked on it with his free hand in the approximate spot his finger-tips should have been.

"Freaky!" Jeff said aloud.

He stood back up and looked down into the device. The blue lights caused strange shadows and made it difficult to see clearly, but it *looked* like his fingers were stretched out into thin, corkscrewing ribbons.

Jeff jerked his hand out of the device when he saw that. He looked at it and shook it vigorously. It looked and felt fine.

"Wow!"

Jeff looked into the opening. It just looked pitch black within the blue glowing ring, but he clearly could not see the table surface which should have been visible.

He brought his hand back to the opening and tentatively pushed his finger-tips back into the opening. This time he watched closely, and this time he could clearly see his fingers 'stretch'. It looked like long, thin banners unfurling in a gently blowing breeze. They stretched and waved and looked to be extended at least 10 inches or more.

This time Jeff laughed.

Amazing.

Looks like Dad came up with something even better than the parabolic mirror. This is really cool, he thought. He wondered what his father's plans were. *Was he planning on selling it as a novelty?*

Jeff wiggled his fingers and watched waves of movement travel through the 'ribbons' his fingers had become.

Awesome!

He withdrew his hand and looked at it again. It still seemed fine.

Jeff ran his eyes from the toroid up the conduits to the control box wondering if he could figure out how it worked.

Not a chance.

It just seemed a jumble of wires switches and knobs. There weren't any labels or instructions. Jeff looked around to see if there were any notes that might explain it. There were pages and pages of notes scattered around the office but nothing Jeff could understand - mostly mathematical equations that just looked like gibberish.

Jeff nosed around some more. He picked up a small laser that had some serious looking coils attached. Jeff considered trying to turn it on but thought better of it.

Then he saw it.

In a dark corner of the office was a much larger version of the toroid he had seen on the table. This one seemed very similar but scaled up to the point that the opening was about three feet in diameter.

Jeff approached it slowly and somewhat nervously.

He got on his knees and began to examine it. Being careful not to touch anything, he moved, twisted, stretched – examined it from as many angles as were possible from his stationary, kneeling position. He could clearly see the floor through the opening in this one just as, he thought, he had seen the table through the smaller one before it had switched itself on.

Jeff made sure he was solidly on the ground. His knees were planted, and he was leaning on his left arm.

He slowly... slowly... *very slowly*... brought his right arm toward the opening.

As the tips of his fingers began to break the plane of the opening, blue lights around the rim, very similar to what he had seen on the smaller one, clicked on with a hum that was similar to but louder than the smaller unit. The otherwise dimly lit office was glowing with the blue light of the odd device.

Beyond the plane defined by the bottom of the blue lights, the interior of the toroid had turned a complete, utter black. He could see his fingertips beginning to stretch and waver in the black field, but they still felt completely normal.

He began to get a little bolder and leaned in closer. He put his hand in slightly farther and his fingers seemed to stretch so much that he couldn't see their tips anymore. They were waving and flapping like ribbons of flesh.

He shifted his weight and continued to lower his arm into the opening. His actual fingers (not the ones that appeared stretched by optical illusion) should have been within inches of the floor.

He got to the point where he was sure that he should be contacting the floor but just kept going. There didn't seem to be anything there anymore. He continued to lean in until the tips of his fingers were at least a foot beyond where the floor should have been.

How the hell is this possible?

He squinted to see what it looked like, but all he could see was his arm turning into a thin, stretched, corkscrewing, waving ribbon stretching into blackness.

Weird, weird, WEIRD.

He withdrew his arm and hand, looked at it... wiggled his fingers... everything seemed completely normal.

He plunged his arm back into the device and leaned into it. He stretched down – clearly far, far past where he should have hit the floor. As he leaned in, part of his face broke the plane, and through his right eye, he began to see streaking colors.

Whoooaa! He jumped back and pulled his head, shoulder and arm completely out as he fell back and skidded uncomfortably on the floor.

He was breathing quickly and shallowly.

He leaned back, sitting on the floor with his weight on his arms and sat for a few moments. He tried to collect himself and catch his breath.

"That was wild," he said out loud.

He looked at the device wondering what it was actually doing. It was still glowing blue and humming rhythmically.

Okay, he thought, *let's see how big of an idiot I actually am.*

He moved back toward the device and looked it over. There was a sturdy metal bar welded to the frame. He wasn't sure if it was supposed to be a handle, but it looked strong enough to serve as one.

Jeff grabbed it firmly. It was solid steel – nearly an inch in diameter – and felt like it could hold hundreds of pounds easily.

With his right hand on the handle, he leaned his head close to the black field. He moved very slowly and cautiously. The top of his head broke the plane first, and when he rolled his eyes toward his forehead, he could see the top part of his head and hair stretching and waving as his fingers and arm had done.

When his eyes entered the field, he again saw the streaking colors, but rather than jumping back, this time he tried to stay calm as he looked around.

It looked like countless multicolored lights streaking past him at thousands of miles per hour. He could see something off in the distance. It was a greenish blur that seemed to be growing at a rapid rate. Within a few seconds, it had grown to the point that it looked like it would envelop his head.

He pulled himself back out.

He looked around his father's office. Everything seemed completely normal. He felt fine – a little dizzy but otherwise clear headed and alert.

Okay. I'm still in one piece... so far.

He was feeling a bit more confident with each step. *It doesn't seem to be doing anything to me.* Jeff patted his head and shoulders, making sure everything was solid and intact. He wasn't sure what he would have done if he found anything out of place.

He put his head back in, this time with more speed and confidence.

Again he saw the streaking lights and approaching green blur. This time his head passed through the green blur and then...

He seemed to come to an abrupt stop. His eyes went in and out of focus, and he realized he was overlooking a vast forest. He was about ten feet from the tops of some tall trees.

He could feel the blood flowing to his head. He looked back to see if he could see back into the office where the rest of his body was, but all he could see was the top of his shoulders emerging through a black circle the same diameter as the inside of the 'hole' he had leaned into. The rest of his body and right arm were 'stretching' into the blackness as far as he could see, and it waved and fluttered like his fingers and arm had from the other side.

He could still feel the handle firmly in his right hand, and he could feel the floor under his knees. Nothing seemed particularly unusual except that instead of looking into his family room, which was below his father's office, he was overlooking a forest.

Which was, of course, impossible.

It must be some kind of amazing hologram, he thought.

And then he did something that, in hindsight, was probably very foolish.

He spat.

As the spittle was falling out of his mouth, he wondered what might happen when spit contacted the complex, delicate circuitry of a sophisticated holographic projection device.

Rather than seeing the wavering image that he thought might result as the spit passed through it and hit the circuit board hidden in the device, it hit some pine needles, the leaves bent under the weight of it. Some of it dripped and slid off onto other needles while some of it fell to the ground far below.

Exactly as it would have on a *real* tree.

Amazing!

He began to actually wonder...

No, that was too crazy...

Wasn't it?

The trees and the forest couldn't actually be... real, could they?

He pulled himself back out of the device and looked around the office.

He pulled a blank piece of paper off of a yellow pad and crumpled it into a ball.

He went back to the ring, grabbed the handle and leaned in again.

He came to a stop, as before, over the forest.

His left arm dangled, holding the paper ball. He moved it around until it lined up over one of the higher, closer branches. He carefully released it, but some wind caught it and blew it away from the branch at which he had been aiming.

While he didn't hit the branch he intended, the paper did hit several other branches as it tumbled, bounced and eventually settled on the forest floor.

Everything it did on the way down had been consistent with what it would have done if Jeff had dropped it onto some real trees in a real forest.

Jeff pulled himself back into the office and sat for several minutes in stunned silence.

Chapter 8:

"And THAT'S why the ducks were in my pants."

Jeff had no idea what was happening in the show he was watching or why the overweight Irishman in the thick, cable sweater had ducks in his pants.

His mind was completely occupied with what he had just seen. *What was that?*

He ran it through his mind again and again trying to make some sense of it. *It couldn't have actually been real... could it? It sure looked real, but how would that be possible? Could it just be an extremely clever illusion? It would have to be very sophisticated. Could it actually be some sort of... portal?*

No... that's crazy.

But what other explanation is there?

Is it more realistic to believe that it's a hologram that is able to interact with objects... and integrate those objects into its system so that not only does the hologram move appropriately as the object passes through but somehow deflects the object while allowing the object to pass through space... that doesn't actually exist... and come to rest in a way that perfectly fits what a person... who has spent his entire life observing the complex interactions of physical objects would expect?

Jeff thought about CGI special effects in movies he had seen, and he thought about how they – no matter how professionally they were rendered – always left subtle clues to the human eye that something just wasn't right. He could never define or say what it was that wasn't right, but his experience told him something wasn't right.

That forest scene was *flawless.*

It looked absolutely perfect. There wasn't anything about it that seemed unnatural.

And what about the floor? How could it just not be there after the device turned on?

Could it really have been a portal?

As crazy as that sounded, it almost seemed more believable than a perfectly rendered illusion.

Could that...

Jeff stopped himself.

He wondered if he was really ready to go there?

Could that... be where Dad is?

Jeff shook his head.

That's just crazy wishful thinking.

Isn't it?

Based on the keys, the last real place that Jeff *knew* his father had been was in that office.

He stood up and began to pace. He was filled with nervous energy. He felt anxious. He felt apprehensive.

He felt... hopeful.

He felt foolish.

Let's start over, he thought to himself. He clasped his hands behind his head.

Dad disappeared mysteriously. He wasn't the sort of person to run away. He didn't have any enemies or anyone who would want to do him harm. Based on the location of his keys, the last place he was known to have been was in his office. There is a mysterious... portal... in his office.

Is it possible... is it likely... that he went into the portal? Do any other explanations make sense? Am I just thinking it's possible because that's what I want to believe?

Jeff sat heavily on the bed and then jumped right back up again. His muscles were like over-wound springs.

Okay, let's assume it's possible. What now? Should I tell someone?

No, they'd just take over and push me aside. What would Dad want? He certainly wouldn't want a bunch of officious busy-bodies climbing all over his marvelous discovery.

Jeff made up his mind.

Chapter 9:

Jeff ran his finger along the labels on the stacks of boxes: Christmas decorations, old toys, Halloween...

Here!

He yanked the box and nearly toppled the whole stack. He steadied the other boxes, and was then able to carefully slide the one he wanted out from under them. He let it drop to the floor in front of him and then, after steadying the rest of the stack so it wouldn't topple, knelt and lifted the lid.

It was as he remembered – filled with rock climbing supplies that Jeff had used many times when he had gone climbing with his father. There were ropes, pulleys, harnesses, carabiners, etc.

Jeff grabbed a long rope and several carabiners.

He half ran, half stumbled back down the attic ladder, folded it back up, pushed the door and let the springs pull it the rest of the way until it slammed loudly.

Jeff cringed. For a very brief moment he expected to hear his father scold him to be more careful.

He made his way back toward the office and suddenly became aware of each footfall. Once he had decided this was what he wanted to do, he couldn't move fast enough, but he also had a fear that something would happen to stop him.

When he was back to the device, he dropped the coil of rope, which fell with a thud beside the device. He examined the bar he had used to secure himself previously.

Seems solid enough, he thought as he tugged on it and visually examine the size, shape and apparent sturdiness. He attached a large carabiner to the 'handle' and then yanked on that to verify the strength of the system. He looped the rope through it and was nearly ready to descend into the portal.

He paused.

I'm going into some strange... zone... that I know nothing about. There is no way to know what to expect. He had been running on adrenaline, but he had the presence of mind to feel he needed something.

A weapon or something to protect myself.

Jeff's father didn't have any guns.

He made his way back out of the office and down the hallway to the bedroom and from there to his closet. He pushed and threw things aside – not at all concerned or even conscious of the mess he was making – until...

Here!

He lifted his aluminum baseball bat. He held it firmly in his right hand and slapped at it with his left hand, trying to feel the solidness and strength of it.

That should give me some protection.... against anyone or anything that isn't too much bigger or stronger... or better armed than me, he thought to himself.

He went back to the office and stood in the doorway trying to think if there was anything else he needed. He looked at the door. *Should I leave it open? No... if I leave it open, Mom might come strolling in.*

He closed and locked the door, dropped the keys in his pocket and then turned off the light.

It seemed pitch black for a moment, but his eyes quickly re-adjusted. He stumbled toward the portal, feeling his way as he went.

Jeff paused as he reached the edge of the device and exhaled forcefully.

Should I really do this? Am I being an idiot? What am I getting myself into?

He had more questions than answers. Part of him realized it wasn't a very good idea, but that was countered by the fact that he had more questions than answers.

Curiosity can be a strong motivator. What kind of world would this be if we always let our minds get in the way of our hearts?

One with a lot less discovery, innovation and achievement.

And one with a lot fewer drunk, naked Facebook and Twitter photos.

Oh, hell... If I keep thinking about it, I'll never do this.

Jeff dipped a toe into the portal which hummed to life. The blue light lit his face. He pulled on the rope, made sure it was secure, tucked the bat under his arm, then threw the free end of the rope into the opening and watched it twist and wave in the blackness.

He stepped into the opening, this time going feet first rather than head first.

He glanced down and could see his body twisting and stretching. That visual was quite disconcerting, so he looked up, focused on the solid feel of the rope and continued lowering himself.

Lights flashed by his head, and within a few moments, he was hanging over the forest. Above him, he could see the rope dangling through a black circle that seemed suspended in the sky.

Jeff looked down and saw the trees below him. He lowered himself through the branches which scratched painfully as he dropped through them. He went slowly, slowly, keeping a good hold on the rope, but it was getting difficult to maintain his concentration as the branches scratched and whipped at him.

When he was about ten feet from the ground, his right foot got caught on a branch and upended him. He desperately tried to keep a hold on the rope, but he was twisted and tangled in a way that made it very difficult to right himself.

The bat slipped, and the thick end hit Jeff in the head with a resounding 'bonk'.

That was enough to throw off the intense concentration he had been using to prevent a fall to the pine-needle blanketed ground below.

Jeff had just enough time to think: *This is going to hurt*, before his back made hard, bone jarring, teeth rattling contact with the ground.

He had the very unpleasant but relatively familiar feeling of having the wind knocked out of himself. He was on the ground, and he clutched his stomach instinctively as he desperately gasped and tried to get air into his lungs.

While he had a familiarity with the sensation, he still couldn't prevent panicking. Colors flashed in his eyes, and he could hear himself making sickening sounds as he struggled to get some air.

His lungs slowly filled, and he began to regain normal breathing. He tried to remain still and calm as he rested on the forest floor. He willed his head to clear and his body to get back to a regularly functioning rhythm.

But before he actually had much time to regain his composure, Jeff saw something moving out of the corner of his eye and tilted his head to get a better look.

About fifteen feet away there was an odd animal. It was about the size of a rabbit and looked somewhat like one but with small ears, a long, naked tail, long hind-legs combined with very short fore-legs and a bi-pedal stance that gave it the general shape of a very small, furry, rodent Tyrannosaurus Rex.

Jeff reached for his bat which was about a foot away from his right hand. As his hand fumbled and then closed around the bat, the rodent saw him and froze.

The two stared at each other, motionless, for a few moments. Jeff heard a sound, looked up and saw something falling from a tree-branch above the rodent.

It looked like a jellyfish – about eighteen inches in diameter – but less regularly shaped than a jellyfish and without tentacles. It almost seemed like a huge amoeba. The thing fell onto the rodent and enveloped it. Jeff could see the frightened animal through the semi-transparent body of the bizarre creature. The rodent struggled violently in an attempt to escape, but it was completely trapped and didn't seem to be making any progress.

After about thirty seconds, its struggling stopped, and

Jeff could see the ghastly look of death on the rodent's face.

Jeff pulled his bat tightly to his chest, raised himself shakily to his feet and then slowly backed away.

Chapter 10:

Now what?

Jeff was surrounded by tall trees. Even though the sun was nearly directly overhead, the shade from the trees made it almost dark where Jeff stood. The non-tree plant-life was minimal. Jeff assumed that the lack of light prevented lush growth.

He could see what appeared to be a clearing a few hundred feet away, and he thought it might be a good idea to head that way. The strange creatures he had seen had creeped him out, and he wanted the comfort of bright day-light.

Maybe that will give me a hint of where to go from there.

He hadn't really thought it all through. He didn't really think that his father would be standing there waving when he arrived, but he didn't really think that he *wouldn't* be there either.

He hadn't really *thought* about anything.

In the back of his mind, he had realized that if he had stopped to think about it too much, he likely wouldn't have done anything. And his heart had been lobbying, VERY HARD, for him to charge ahead. It was as if his heart had kicked open the door to his brain and dropped a satchel filled with bundled hundred-dollar bills on the desk: *'I'm sure we can come to some kind of understanding on this.'*

When he was fifty feet from the clearing, he froze. He saw some movement at the base of a nearby tree. He clenched his bat tightly and tried to get a better look. From a hollow in the tree, emerged a HUGE beetle – two feet in diameter with sharp, six-inch mandibles. The beetle climbed out of the tree and headed away from him into the clearing.

Then another beetle emerged and followed the first... then another and another...

Soon there were twenty to thirty very big beetles all

marching in formation into the clearing.

Jeff watched silently hoping they would get well out in front of him. He wanted to keep an eye on them. He was a good bit larger than them, but those pinchers looked like they could do some damage. And if they ganged up on him...

Jeff had seen nature shows in which ants had taken down grasshoppers many times their size with some well-coordinated teamwork. He shuddered at the thought.

When the lead beetle was about one-hundred feet into the clearing, Jeff saw a large shadow pass over the line, then another.

Jeff looked up to see what was causing the shadow, but the trees were blocking his view. He cautiously edged closer to the clearing.

Holy...

Circling the line of beetles were three huge... *birds?* They had wingspans of nine feet.

There also seemed to be something unusual about their heads. Jeff squinted into the sun and saw that their heads didn't look like bird heads but looked more like badger or weasel heads.

The birds swooped and snatched beetles from the line. The formation scattered and some of the beetles headed back toward Jeff.

Jeff began to panic.

The beetles were running fast, erratically, and spreading out in all directions.

Jeff started backing quickly away but tried to keep a watch on as many of the beetles and birds as possible. Within seconds though, he had beetles in front of him, behind him and on all sides.

Jeff saw one of the birds swoop down and snatch a beetle just at the tree line, but the birds didn't seem to pursue the beetles beyond that line.

After a few more minutes, the beetles that hadn't been eaten found hiding places. The birds went off out of sight, and the forest was calm again.

Jeff stood for a few moments weighing his options and began to think this might be an example of discretion being the better part of valor.

He wasn't sure what wetting his pants and crying like a little girl would have been the better part of.

I think it's time to go back and re-think this whole thing.

He began retracing his steps to where he had dropped. He had paid close attention to the path he had taken, and he had a good sense of direction.

Crap!

He thought he was headed in the right direction, but everything started to look the same.

He resumed his panic.

He was tempted to begin running, but he realized that would be very foolish. Instead, he continued slowly and methodically while trying to convince himself he had a clue where he was going.

After about five minutes – that felt more like twenty – he could see the spot where he had landed.

There it is!

The rope was dangling down the side of the tree. Jeff followed the rope with his eyes, and he could see it was hanging through a black circle in the sky.

I wish I had thought this through a little better.

He could climb most of the way by finding footholds on branches and using the rope to balance and guide himself, but there was a gap of at least ten feet from the top of the tree to the portal. *That will be a tough climb.*

Jeff was a good climber, but the rope was thin and not knotted.

Just relax, take your time, Jeff told himself. *I can lock off and take a break if I need to. I can just inch my way up if it's too hard to do it all at once.*

His stomach turned over as he thought about himself hanging there in the sky, far above the ground with nothing but rope. He felt sweat bead on his forehead even though the temperature was cool.

He decided that the longer he thought about it, the harder it would be, so he grabbed the rope and began to make his way up the tree.

He had the bat tucked under one arm but quickly realized he couldn't hold the bat and climb easily at the same time. He dropped the bat and watched it fall with some trepidation. The bat had given him some sense of comfort, but it was holding him back.

For a moment, he thought about his mom and how she wouldn't be happy about replacing the bat, but then he wondered why his brain occupied itself with such mundane details when his very life might be in danger.

He climbed quickly and within a relatively short time, he was nearing the top of the tree. He paused a moment to catch his breath. He had a good view of the portal now, and as he looked at it, he saw something that made his face go white.

The black circle seemed to be getting... *smaller!* Jeff squinted and tried to make sure his eyes weren't playing tricks on him, but the longer he looked, the surer he became that the portal seemed to be closing and tightening around the rope.

After a few moments, the black circle was basically gone, and the rope seemed to just be hanging in the air.

Jeff stared.

He wasn't sure what this meant, but he was getting very nervous. He hoped that, when he got to the end of the rope, he could coax the portal to open again as he had opened it on the other end by breaking the plane.

But I can't be sure that will work.

He continued to stare at the end of the rope – just hanging there.

As he watched, he saw the end of the rope begin to... *glow.*

Then it began to spark.

Jeff had an idea where things were headed, and he got

a firm footing on a strong branch. No sooner had he done that than the rope fell and hung limply from his hand..

He pulled the rope up and examined the end. The fibers were melted and lumpy.

"Idiot!" Jeff said out loud.

He hadn't even thought about what would happen when the machine turned off. It had turned itself off before when he had left the office and then came back. It must only stay open for a limited time. *Probably uses a lot of power, so it has an automatic shut-off,* Jeff thought.

He dropped down and sat on the branch on which he had been standing.

For a while, he just sat there and stared.

After a few minutes, he was shaken out of his daze by a long, eerie, moaning howl coming from somewhere in the forest.

Chapter 11:

Jeff paused about five feet from the ground and scanned for anything that might be moving. His stomach twisted as he remembered the 'amoeba', and he twisted his head back to squint upward through the branches.

Nothing.

At least nothing I can recognize as dangerous.

But what might be dangerous here?

Are there plants that can come to life? Or maybe they just kill more mundanely by exuding toxins.

He pulled his hand off of the branch and looked at it.

He shivered and thought about the time his father told him: "There are very few things as frightening as the unknown."

I'll go crazy if I imagine everything that could happen.

He hopped onto the ground and snatched up his bat as quickly as he could manage. At least it gave him some sense of security. *Hey, if I can imagine all types of irrational danger, I've got a right to put some irrational trust in a piece of aluminum*, he reasoned.

He scanned the forest. He couldn't see anything other than trees and underbrush, but he could hear sounds. *Insects? Birds?* They didn't quite sound like anything he had ever heard, but they didn't sound particularly unusual either.

Like the sounds he'd expect in a forest, just a little off.

He began walking slowly, sweeping his eyes left, right, up, down obsessively.

Where do I go from here?

He didn't have many choices. *It seems to be: a) Head into the forest to face God-knows-what.*

Or...

b) Head into the clearing to face God-knows-what.

42

He decided on the clearing but wasn't sure if that was the wisest thing. After all, he'd be more exposed out there. He hoped he was too big for the 'birds' to make a meal out of him, but he wasn't sure.

There were times, back home, when he had 'hoped' Alicia Keys would show up in his room – naked, bearing Ho-Ho's and Vanilla coke – and offer to give him a back rub while she sang gently in his ear.

That had never happened.

But he knew he'd feel more comfortable in the clearing than in the forest. He might have less cover in which to hide, but so would predators.

It's a very strange and uncomfortable feeling to have no idea where I fall on the food chain.

Jeff stopped.

There was a large hole, about six feet in diameter ten feet ahead. He had the uncomfortable feeling it was a burrow of an extremely large animal of some sort.

He considered moving away as quickly as possible, but his curiosity got the better of him. He kept his distance but stretched up on his toes to see if he could see anything in the hole.

There was a flash of movement, and the next thing Jeff knew, an ENORMOUS snake was emerging from the hole. Its head was over three feet in diameter.

Jeff jumped back and adrenaline shot into his system. He took off at a run – faster than he ever imagined he was capable.

Over his shoulder, he saw the snake completely clear the hole. It was shorter than he would have imagined with its body about a third the length he would have expected from the size of its head.

Also – and this was a detail that Jeff was too distracted to notice at that particular moment – it had three pairs of short, stubby, lizard-like legs. It moved like a snake, but the legs helped propel and steady it at certain points. Other times they tucked up and out of the way -

like an alligator's legs did when it swam.

Jeff realized that it was gaining fast, and he didn't have a chance of out-running it. He had no choice but to *try* to fight and decided the quicker and more forcefully he acted, the better.

He turned to face it, raised his bat – the snake was nearly on him. His arm tensed, and he brought the bat down with all the force he could manage on the snake's nose.

The bat made contact with a satisfyingly powerful impact. The snake shook, lurched and backed off several feet, taken by surprise and seemingly slightly dazed.

The two looked at each other.

Jeff was trying to stay focused. He was breathing hard, and the exertion and adrenaline were giving him a feeling of light-headedness. Time seemed to slow down as each of them considered the other – both nearly motionless. Jeff was right at the edge of the clearing, and he could see shadows of birds but tried not to let that distract him.

Then the snake began to move. It moved its head to Jeff's left but kept more distance than it had the last time. Jeff had the bat raised over his right shoulder in a batting stance ready to swing, but he didn't want to swing until the snake was in range. He kept his left shoulder pointed at the snake's head focused intently on every move.

The snake could move fast, but Jeff took some comfort in the idea that a baseball could also move pretty fast too while presenting a much smaller target.

Though most baseballs lacked enormous fangs.

The snake pulled back and then moved slowly around on Jeff's right side. Jeff followed its movements keeping his left shoulder pointed at his target.

The snake's mouth was open slightly, and Jeff could see rows of hundreds of six inch long teeth. He grimaced as he imagined for a moment what would happen if those teeth sunk into his flesh.

The snake moved back to the left...

Then the right.

Then left again.

Then it LURCHED!

Jeff acted instinctively as the snake came at him extremely fast with mouth open. He smashed it as hard as he could in the mouth and several teeth cracked as the bat struck. Again the snake retreated but only enough to get safely out of range.

Jeff didn't know how long he could keep it up. He already felt *exhausted*. It didn't seem like he was doing much, but the adrenaline and hyper-focus were wearing him out.

He backed into the clearing, hoping that the snake might prefer the cover of the trees and not follow. Jeff tried not to get distracted with thoughts of what might be out in the clearing that would frighten the snake.

The snake followed him into the field. It was holding back a little – apparently still feeling some pain from their last encounter – but it held within about 10 feet of Jeff.

The dance started again.

The snake moved slowly from one side to the other, and Jeff matched each of his moves.

Jeff began to try to steal quick glances to get a read of his options. He was afraid that if this became a marathon, the snake could easily outlast him. Jeff was on the verge of exhaustion, but the snake, while maybe in some pain, wasn't exerting much energy at all.

Jeff noted a few trees with low hanging branches that he thought he might be able to scale if he could knock the snake out or distract it.

Can snakes climb trees?

Can lizards climb trees?

Can this... thing climb trees?

I'd assume 'yes' on all three counts.

Jeff felt a wave of shear panic wash over him then quickly disappear as his mind stopped drifting and focused back on the urgent, immediate concern.

The snake seemed to be more stationary than it had been. Jeff wondered if it realized time was on its side and there was no rush.

Jeff felt his muscles start to relax for a moment, and he forced himself to snap back into focus. Fatigue and a sense of hopelessness were beginning to crowd out his sense of urgency.

The snake reared back and prepared for another attack.

But held.

Jeff got a sudden sick feeling that the snake was afraid of something.

Something *behind* Jeff.

A shadow fell over him, and before he could react, something grabbed him and jerked him violently backward.

Chapter 12:

It wasn't a painful or tearing attack as if something latched onto him with teeth or claws but more like something relatively soft had wrapped around and then pulled him – violently but without causing any damage – away from the snake with a sudden acceleration.

Jeff was traveling backward at about forty miles per hour. His heels skimmed the ground, bouncing as he went.

Then Jeff heard something that seemed impossible.

A girl's voice.

"Hang on kid. We got you," she said.

Jeff saw that the snake had gotten over its initial fear and was in pursuit. But Jeff was moving away far faster than the snake could travel, so the distance between them was growing.

Jeff craned his neck around, and saw that the girl had her arms wrapped around him. She was sitting in an open flying vehicle that was moving sideways as it hovered three feet above the ground. Jeff was pinned against the side of the car – held there by the firm grip the girl had on him.

"Give us a minute to get far enough away," she said, "and then we'll stop so you can hop in."

"Thanks!" Jeff said. It seemed far too little, but he was at something of a loss for words at that moment.

When there was a good, safe distance between them and the snake, they stopped and Jeff scrambled into the passenger compartment behind the two front seats. He saw that the girl – actually 'young woman', an attractive twentyish year old – was in the left-front seat, and there was a boy, about Jeff's age, to her right. The young woman had some sort of steering yoke in front of her, but the boy seemed to have a hand on the yoke and was steering from the passenger seat. Once her hands were free, she took the controls back, and the vehicle lurched upward. They picked up some SERIOUS speed and put a very comfortable distance between the vehicle and the snake.

"Give me a minute to find a good place to set down, so we can hear each other," she shouted over her shoulder.

Chapter 13:

After a very brief flight, the vehicle settled down on top of a ledge overlooking a fast moving stream. Beyond that was a vast, rocky arid area that contrasted with the lushness of the forest they had just left.

"Nahima," the young woman introduced herself, "and this is my brother, Baldwin."

"Jeff."

"Did your mobile break down or something?" Nahima asked.

By 'mobile', Jeff assumed she meant something similar to the flying vehicle they were in. It was a simple, open, four-seat vehicle with a minimal body, but it sure seemed to move.

"That was UNTAMED!" Baldwin exclaimed. "I can't imagine fighting a hexapod serpent with a... metal club."

They seemed to both speak with a slight accent that Jeff couldn't place, nothing dramatic, but some of their pronunciations seemed just a bit unusual.

He reached for Jeff's bat. "May I?"

"Sure." Jeff tried not to look nervous as Baldwin examined his bat. He had no idea where he was or who these people were, or how their society treated crazy people. He decided it would be best to try to blend in if possible and find out as much as he could about where he was before letting on that he had come from a hole in the sky.

He noticed that Nahima and Baldwin wore very simple, plain clothes. He didn't imagine that his blue T-shirt looked particularly unusual, but he suspected his jeans and sneakers looked very foreign to them.

The bat was certainly something that Baldwin had never seen, and he studied it admiringly.

"Of course given a choice between a hexapod serpent

and Nahima's driving..."

Nahima PUNCHED Baldwin on the shoulder before he could finish the thought. Jeff was reasonably sure it was a good natured punch, but it nearly knocked Baldwin out of his seat.

"Owww..." Baldwin said smiling as he rubbed his arm. "Are you taking hormones or something? You punch way too hard for a girl."

She raised her fist again, and Baldwin cringed.

"It doesn't take much to beat your scrawny back-end," she taunted but never threw the second punch.

Jeff was glad for the distraction. His mind was racing trying to think of what he should tell them when they pressed him for details of just *why* he was out there battling a snake-creature with a metal club.

He had absolutely no idea where he was. It looked basically like Earth, but the creatures he saw in the forest certainly weren't from any part of Earth he knew. He was talking to two humans who spoke perfect English, but the flying car certainly seemed a sign that they weren't in Oshkosh.

If I tell them the truth, will they assume I'm crazy? Or worse, will they actually believe I'm from another dimension and fear I'm the opening wave of an invading army? I can't imagine I'm particularly threatening, but it seems if I tell the truth I stand a good chance of ending up in a government lab getting an anal probe... as a best case scenario.

But, he had a feeling.

He had a strong feeling he could trust those two people who had saved his life. It was more than just seeing that they had kind faces. It was almost as if he had a voice in the back of his head saying: *Trust them.*

Jeff shook his head to clear out any unwanted voices. It didn't seem the time or place to go loopy.

He ran through several options in his head.

Seems like the less I say, the better. But how can I avoid the obvious questions? Can I just say I don't want to talk? Would that seem rude, or worse, evasive?

He realized time was quickly running out and felt he needed to come up with something very soon.

Amnesia! That might work.

"So why were you out there?" Nahima asked as if on cue.

"Uhhhhhh..." Jeff did his best to conjure a vacant, confused expression. "I'm..." He paused and pretended to be deep in thought, then he tried to look nervous and apprehensive. "I'm not sure."

He began to fidget nervously. He found the nervousness wasn't very difficult to fake. "I... I mean... I... can't think of who I am... I mean... I know my name's Jeff, but I can't remember anything else... I can't remember where I live or who my parents are..." He looked off toward the horizon and pretended to be trying to regain his lost memories.

Baldwin and Nahima looked at each other with open mouths.

"Whooaah..." Baldwin broke the silence. "That's weird." He turned toward Nahima. "What should we do? Should we take him to the hospital?"

Jeff cringed. He hadn't thought of that. Once he was in the hospital, how would he get out? Would they hold him until someone claimed him?

"I don't know." Nahima seemed to sense Jeff's discomfort. "Maybe we could take him home first... see what Dad thinks."

Chapter 14:

The vehicle was quiet, smooth and fast. It glided, seemingly effortlessly, over an arid, rocky landscape. There was almost no vegetation: Some dry brush and scattered weeds, but other than that, not much more than rock and dry, cracked dirt. Jeff could see what looked like a city in the distance through a bluish haze.

As they got closer, Jeff realized that the bluish haze was some sort of energy *wall*. There were thousands of thin, metal poles stretching to the left and right as far as Jeff could see. The poles were hundreds – maybe thousands – of feet high. Each one was about 100 feet from the next, and between each pole was a light blue, mostly transparent wall of energy.

Nahima slowed the car, pushed a few buttons on her dash, and the energy wall between the two poles closest to them disappeared. She flew through the opening. Jeff looked over his shoulder as they flew through, and he and saw the energy field re-appear between the poles after they had passed.

Jeff thought about that for a moment. In a way he was glad to see something between him and the forest.

But am I locked in now... locked in... where?

Just inside the wall, there was a dramatic change in landscape. Outside the wall, the land was rocky and dry, but that had given way to farmland. The crops weren't as lush and green as those that Jeff was used to in New Jersey. Jeff saw some sprinklers going, but they didn't seem to be able to give the crops as much water as they needed.

They passed over farm houses and something that looked like a fairly typical rural area – similar to what Jeff was used to back home. The most noticeable difference he saw was that the buildings seemed to use rounder shapes in their architecture rather than the rectangular buildings and straight lines Jeff was used to. There were some wheeled vehicles – some looked like futuristic tractors and some looked more like futuristic cars. Jeff took some comfort in seeing good old-fashioned wheels, but he could also see other flying vehicles visible in the distance.

As they closed the distance between themselves and the city, Jeff could see that the taller buildings toward the center of the city were also more rounded than those back home.

At a distance Jeff estimated to be about five to ten miles past the energy wall and roughly half-way to the tall buildings he could see there was a dense collection of small buildings. *The suburban area,* Jeff assumed.

Nahima slowed as she approached a domed house. There was a driveway and what Jeff recognized as a garage door even though it didn't look like a typical garage door. It was wide enough for four or more cars, but rather than going up, it slid into the ground to open. Nahima pulled into the huge garage and the craft settled to the ground. Jeff saw that there were two other vehicles. One vehicle had wheels and looked like a futuristic but not otherwise unusual car. The other one was resting on landing 'feet', and Jeff assumed it flew.

"Well, we made it," Baldwin said. "I always feel fortunate when I can say that after a flight with Nahima." He opened his door, hopped out and made an exaggerated gesture of kissing the ground.

Nahima shot him a dirty look. "You just wait until the next time we're out. I'll show you how much fun flying with me can be." Her face broke into an evil, eerie grin.

"You don't have to convince me," Baldwin said. "I've seen it before."

"But you've never seen me *really* trying to scare you until you plooch your pants," she said, still grinning.

"Next time, you better bring some diapers."

Jeff fumbled with the door latch. It was an unfamiliar design, but after some fiddling, he felt a lever move slightly and there was a 'click'. The door opened slightly. Jeff pushed it enough to get out and then - following Nahima and Baldwin's lead – gently closed it again.

He realized he still had the bat in his hand but thought it might seem rude to walk into someone's house carrying a baseball bat – particular a society that only knew it as a 'metal club' – so he tossed it back into the car.

Jeff looked around, fascinated by what he was seeing. The garage looked similar to a typical garage, but there were subtle differences. There were various tools and vehicles, but while they were somewhat recognizable, they didn't look *exactly* like any tools or vehicles he had seen before.

Nahima and Baldwin spoke perfect English, but there was that subtle accent. He had also seen some writing on signs, and he could see some writing on some of the objects in the garage. Everything was in English. Some of the spelling seemed a little odd, and the letters somewhat stylized but nothing dramatic.

How is that possible? Jeff knew he wasn't in an episode of Star Trek in which completely alien races just, somehow, speak English.

This was a completely foreign world, and there was no logical way they should speak the same language as Jeff.

There had to be some connection between this world and Jeff's world, *but how can that be possible?* Jeff was anxious to find out as much as he could about where he was, but he was being patient.

Best to just play dumb until I know a little more about where the heck I am.

Chapter 15:

"We're home, Dad!" Nahima announced as they entered the house.

"Out in a minute... " Jeff heard a man's voice say from another room.

Nahima gestured to a large, soft piece of furniture that had flowing curves. Jeff assumed it was a type of couch, and he sat. It was *amazingly* comfortable. Jeff felt like he was melting into it.

When Jeff had gone to Italy several years ago, he remembered thinking: *So this is how food is supposed to taste.*

As he sat on that couch, he thought: *So this is how furniture is supposed to feel.*

He made a point of keeping his eyes open, because he had a feeling that if he closed them, he'd be asleep and drooling shortly. He was physically, and mentally *exhausted.*

Jeff looked around the room. The design of everything was foreign. Shapes and contours seemed different than what he knew. He noticed a number of pieces of art that had 'oval' themes. There were sculptures, paintings, sketches, and many of them seemed to feature ovals as central figures.

There was an *extremely* loud belch from the other room and then the man's voice: "Ha! How was that? I'd rate that a good ninety-four or ninety-five. What do you think?"

Baldwin and Nahima smirked at one another.

"Dinner's in about fifteen minutes," the voice continued, then the man put his head through the doors. He had a huge grin and was wearing an oversized, red hat.

His grin dropped.

His face began to turn the shade of his hat when he saw Jeff. "Oh, I didn't know we had a guest."

The man quickly pulled the hat from his head and

threw it back into the room he had come from – which Jeff guessed was the kitchen. He was an unremarkable man – medium height and on the heavy side of medium weight-wise. He looked like he might have been reasonably athletic at some point in his life, but age had softened him.

Still, there was something powerful about him that belied his physical appearance. Something in his eyes that made Jeff feel there was an intensity just below the surface.

The man wiped his hands on his apron and walked toward Jeff. "Artimus," he said as he extended a hand. "We'd probably have to wait quite a while for my kids to introduce me. They apparently weren't raised very well." He winked.

Jeff rose and reached for his hand. As they shook, he thought to himself: *They shake hands just like we do. Their culture seems very similar to ours.*

"Jeff," he introduced himself.

"Jeff has sort of a problem we wanted to talk to you about," Nahima said.

"Oh," Artimus' eyebrows raised in an expression of curiosity. "How can I help?"

Once again, similar to the feeling he had regarding Baldwin and Nahima, Jeff had a strong feeling that he could trust Artimus. Still, he thought it best to be cautious.

"Well... uh...," Jeff tried to think what he should say. "I seem to have some sort of amnesia. I can't really remember anything about myself except my name. Everything else is just... blank."

Artimus' face showed sincere concern. "Nothing at all? Can you remember anything about your parents? Your neighborhood? A street or school?"

Jeff paused to make it appear he was considering all these questions very carefully.

"No... nothing... I can't remember anything before fighting the hexapod serpent and then getting picked up by

Nahima and Baldwin."

Jeff saw Nahima and Baldwin cringe and realized he said something he shouldn't have.

Artimus turned his attention to them. "You went to the forest?" he asked with raised eyebrows.

Nahima rolled her eyes but also seemed a little defensive. "We're fine *Dad.*" She put an unpleasant emphasis on 'Dad' that made Jeff uncomfortable. "We can take care of ourselves."

Artimus seemed a bit frustrated but measured. "I know you can take care of yourselves, but most people would be horrified to think I would let a thirteen and eighteen year old go to the forest alone. Anymore, it seems like most people are horrified at the thought of a thirty year old going there."

Jeff was a little surprised to hear that Baldwin and Nahima were so young. They both looked a little older than that to him, but then he realized a 'year' might not be the same as the year he knew. *Maybe it's a little longer.*

Or maybe they weren't quite human and had slightly different aging.

"Anyway, that's not really important now." Artimus turned his attention back to Jeff. "Jeff, can you think of anything at all that could help? Do you have any identification or anything else with you that might help us out?"

Jeff made a display of patting his pockets and then slowly shook his head. He noticed Artimus looking at his jeans and shoes with some curiosity.

"Those are unusual pants and shoes," he said. "You guys are more up on the fashions than I am," he said to Nahima and Baldwin. "Any idea where someone might get clothes like that?"

They both shook their heads.

"Wait!" Baldwin said as he seemed to remember something, "He also had a really strange metal club." He jumped up. "Did you leave it in the car?"

Jeff nodded, and Baldwin ran off to the garage.

Jeff squirmed uncomfortably. He wasn't ready for them to know the truth – that he was an alien from another dimension – but he was afraid he might have some trouble explaining these things. He took some comfort that he didn't really have to explain anything. As long as they believed he had amnesia, he could always be an alien from another dimension with amnesia. And if didn't tell them he was an alien from another dimension but they made that leap...

Well... who would be crazy then?

All the while he had that voice in the back of his head: *It's okay. You can trust them.* But he still thought it best to be cautious. After all, how did he know he could trust the voice in his head? He considered that more harm than good typically came from people listening to the voices in their heads.

Baldwin returned with the bat and showed it to Artimus.

Artimus examined it carefully, looking down his nose and pursing his lips with an expression of concentration: "Louisville Slugger TPX." He mispronounced 'Louisville' badly.

"Do you have any idea what this is?" he asked Jeff.

Jeff shook his head slowly. "I don't know. It seems sort of familiar, but I just don't know."

"I'm sure your parents must be terribly worried," Artimus said. "I mean you're welcome to stay with us. That's not a problem, but somewhere your parents are probably wondering where you are."

The four of them sat quietly for a few moments.

"I guess I should call the police," Artimus said after a while.

Jeff cringed and Artimus seemed to recognize his apprehension.

"I'll tell you what," Artimus said. "I won't haul you down there and leave you stuck there filling out paperwork all night. I know a few people at headquarters. I can call, let them know you're here, and find out if they've heard from your parents. If they have, great, if not maybe they will. Then your parents will at least know where to find you.

"Tomorrow, when the city offices are open, I'll run your retina through the identification system, and that should tell us who you are."

"Good... that sounds great." Jeff was relieved, but he knew that they'd soon find he didn't match anyone. He wasn't sure what would happen then.

It seemed that he had at least bought himself some time. He doubted that anyone would have reported him missing at the police station.

Jeff realized that there was something *very* important that he needed to address. With everything that was going on, he had nearly forgotten.

"Ummm, may I use your bathroom?" he asked a bit sheepishly.

Chapter 16:

This might get interesting, Jeff thought as he looked around.

Like much of what he had seen since they passed the barrier into the populated area, the bathroom looked familiar, yet the design was unique and incorporated flowing lines and curves that were much less harsh than those designs with which Jeff was familiar.

The sink looked like something one might see in a magazine featuring exotic, modern design.

But the toilet...

This might require some thought, Jeff mused.

It was similar to the toilets he knew but curved into a shape something like a saddle rather than the flat seats he was used to.

The big problem at the moment was that the lid appeared to be part of it.

He reached around the bowl but couldn't find any edge, and the lid seemed solidly fused to the bowl.

He looked around and found three buttons on the wall. One had a symbol that looked like a little whirlpool – *flush,* he reasoned. Then there was one with a symbol that looked like a Pringles potato chip and another that looked like the same potato chip but with a large hole cut out of the center.

Now we're getting somewhere.

He assumed that the 'potato chip' was the lid, and the chip with the hole was the seat.

He pushed the chip, and the lid... *disappeared.* The lid didn't seem to lift or slide, it just seemed to waver and disappear like it was some sort of energy field.

It had felt perfectly solid when he had been feeling for an edge.

Jeff pushed the button again, and the lid re-appeared.

There was a visual distortion of the air around the lid when it re-appeared. It seemed that it was some sort of energy field, but once it was in place, it looked and felt like a solid piece of plastic.

"Cool!" Jeff said out loud. As he pushed the button again and watched it disappear once more.

Then he pushed the 'seat' button and a blue shield appeared covering the upper lip of the bowl. Like the lid, it seemed to have formed from an energy field, but it felt solid.

I don't know which is cooler, the flying car or this, Jeff thought, smiling to himself. *I guess bacteria can't grow on surfaces... that don't actually exist.*

He instinctively looked over his shoulder, fearing for a moment that his hosts would witness his fascination with the toilet and suspect something was up, but the door was closed behind him.

After he had figured things out satisfactorily and completed the important matters, he found Baldwin who showed him to a place at a casually set table in the kitchen.

Knife, fork, spoon, Jeff noticed.

How is it that some things were so similar to what I know and yet...

That's it!! Jeff thought. *I must be in the future.* He wasn't sure why it took him so long to figure it out. He was thrown by the forest, but what about the forest? Why would there be such unusual creatures in the future? In the time it would take them to evolve, even under extraordinary circumstances, human society would have changed much more dramatically than what he was seeing ... *wouldn't it?*

Well it was at least something to work with. *Maybe I can find some more clues.*

Artimus put some steaming trays on the table and took his seat.

Jeff sat and waited. *What's the etiquette here? Will they say grace? Will I be expected to do anything?* He began to fidget nervously.

"Let us give thanks," Artimus said cheerfully.

Jeff bowed his head but peeked and saw that everybody else had heads up and eyes open. He kept his head somewhat bowed but tried not to make it too obvious.

"Lord, thank you for this hearty meal, and please guide us in best serving those who need our help... particularly in these difficult times."

That was it – *short and sweet.*

Artimus handed a tray of what appeared to be meat to Baldwin who forked out a generous portion for himself before passing it to Nahima.

"I apologize," Artimus said, "but since Nahima and Baldwin's mother passed away, I'm afraid I've been forced to fumble around in the kitchen.

"It may not be good, but nobody has died ... yet... Maybe a little violent vomiting but no deaths." He laughed, then his face turned mock serious as he leaned over to Nahima and said, in a stage whisper: "That Peterson kid didn't really count, did he?"

"No... no..." Nahima said, "He was scrawny. It wasn't because the food was that bad. He just didn't have enough body mass. Why I'll bet he wasn't much heavier than Jeff here."

They all looked at Jeff, and then the whole table broke out in loud, hearty laughter.

"Don't worry," Nahima said. "Dad really is a great cook."

Jeff took a bite of some type of meat in a gravy and it really was delicious – very soft and light but with some subtle, interesting flavors.

"This is one of the best things I've ever tasted," he said honestly.

Chapter 17:

"I hate to impose..." Jeff apologized.

"Don't worry about it," Baldwin said with a grin. "I don't mind. It's sort of fun to have someone else around." He picked up several books that were spread over the bed Jeff would be using. Jeff looked around, curious about what Baldwin would do with the books. The room was a mess and there didn't seem to be much empty space.

As if in answer to Jeff's unspoken question, Baldwin dropped them loudly and sloppily on the floor. "Besides, Dad's a little easier to get along with when we have a guest."

"Really? He seemed like he was relaxed and easy-going to me," Jeff said a bit surprised.

"Don't get me wrong. He's a great guy... he just expects a lot. Sometimes I feel like I'll never be as smart as he is, and I worry I'll let him down."

Jeff could relate to that. He often thought his own father was so smart that he wondered if he could ever live up to the legacy. There was a strange pressure being the son of a brilliant man. 'Are you going to be a physicist too?' his father's friends would ask when they met him. 'He's one of the smartest people I've ever met, and he's always telling me how bright you are.'

Jeff cringed as he thought of those conversations. He should have been flattered, but it always felt like too much pressure at that point in his life. He was just worried about passing algebra, and he couldn't ever imagine doing the great things people seemed to expect of him.

I'm letting myself get distracted. This is the perfect opportunity to find out more about where I am. I've got amnesia after all, so some stupid questions should be excusable.

"Uhhhh," he began. "This is going to sound like a stupid question, but what year is it?"

Baldwin laughed then started to turn red. "Oh, I'm sorry. I shouldn't laugh. It just seems... weird to not even know what year it is. It's 545."

545? That doesn't sound like the future. Unless they had changed the way they count years.

Jeff tried to think of other ways he could get information without pushing it.

"Do you have a globe?"

"Sure." Baldwin slid some books aside on his desk and pushed a button. A projection of a twelve-inch diameter globe appeared above the desk, and Baldwin gave it a good spin. Even though it seemed to be a projection, it reacted to his touch. "Lights off," Baldwin said, and the lights dimmed until the only light was coming from the globe, illuminating Jeff and Baldwin's faces with an eerie, shifting light.

Jeff – slowly and a little nervously – reached toward it. He couldn't feel it, but it could *feel* him.

It stopped spinning as soon as his hand hit what would have been its surface. He moved his hand, imagining it was a solid globe, and it moved with his hand.

It was clearly not the Earth. The ratio of land to water was roughly the same as Earth's, and there were two large land masses on opposite sides of the globe - similar to Earth, but the shapes were completely different.

There seemed to be areas and regions listed but not the sort of dense cities that one would see on a map of the United States, for example.

Jeff wondered how much he could get away with asking before Baldwin got suspicious, but his curiosity was beginning to overwhelm his cautiousness.

"Where... uhhhh, where are we?" Jeff tensed a bit, hoping Baldwin wouldn't question if there wasn't something more than amnesia going on.

Baldwin just shook his head and tried to suppress a laugh. "You really are out of it, aren't you?"

Jeff nodded sheepishly and was beginning to feel less

nervous about being discovered and more guilty for his deception.

"Here," Baldwin put his finger on an area labeled 'Caesurmia' near the eastern edge of one of the land masses.

"Zoom in." He said and the globe complied. The image never stretched beyond the boundaries of the original globe, but it flattened into a map as it zoomed in. Baldwin touched the edge of the image when it was where he wanted, and it stopped zooming.

Jeff stared at the detailed image of a sprawling city surrounded by suburbs which were encircled by farmland. Jeff could see what he assumed was the arid area they had flown over, and the forest beyond that. It was an amazingly detailed three-dimensional image – it didn't look like a photograph or a map – it seemed to actually have all of the buildings, mountains etc. and even trees and shrubbery in relief with perfect proportions. Jeff felt like he was a giant actually looking down at a real landscape.

"The forest," Jeff said. "Does anyone live out there?"

"A few people," Baldwin said. "Most people live in Caesurmia and Doclotnury, but there are some people who live out in the forest, scattered around. I couldn't imagine that – too dangerous." Baldwin suppressed an involuntary shiver.

"Yeah, I noticed," Jeff commented.

"You don't have any idea why you were out there?" Baldwin asked.

Jeff shook his head and tried to change the subject. "Doclotnury. You mentioned Doclotnury. Where's that?"

"Zoom out." Baldwin said, and the globe went back to full zoom. Baldwin turned it a quarter turn, and Jeff could see 'Doclotnury' clearly labeled toward the western edge of the same land mass that Caesurmia was on.

Jeff reached out and rocked the globe back and forth, getting a feel for it before rotating it around to the other land mass on the opposite side.

"Are there people living here?" He turned the globe around and pointed to the land mass on the opposite side of the globe.

Baldwin laughed. "No, the pheerions live over there. I don't think they'd like the idea of humans trying to live there."

"Pheerions?" Jeff wondered who, or *what* would dominate a continent so that this technologically advanced society wouldn't consider living there.

"You don't even know what a pheerion is?" Baldwin grinned slightly devilishly. "Image – pheerion," Baldwin said, and the globe blurred and turned into a holographic image.

Jeff gaped. In his mind, he was stumbling backward and clutching his chest Fred Sanford-like, but in reality, he just stared with his mouth open.

The image was the creature he had been seeing in his dreams.

Chapter 18:

Jeff was in a daze as he prepared for bed. He had been having trouble sleeping back home because he had been dreaming about a terrifying creature, *and he had just seen a holographic image of that creature.*

There had been moments since he arrived that he considered this whole thing could be a dream, but he kept coming back to fact that it simply wasn't. When Jeff did dream, he sometimes couldn't tell if he was dreaming or not, but when he was awake, there was no ambiguity.

When he was awake, there was always a clear lucidity. He always knew where he was and where he had been. He could see and feel and smell everything clearly, and that's how he felt now.

The events of the past half-day had been so unbelievable, it almost seemed that it had to be a dream, but his clear perception of his surroundings left him absolutely certain that he was awake and fully aware of what was going on around him.

Could boredom actually lead to madness? Was it possible for one's brain to become so disinterested with the mundanity of life that it started dreaming while the person was still awake?

"There's no school this week, so you can hang around with me tomorrow," Baldwin said. He seemed to be enjoying the idea of having an unexpected companion. "Dad will check at work and see if he can track down your family."

Artimus had taken an image of Jeff's retina and was planning to run it through the computer the next day. Jeff realized he'd have to come clean soon, but he wanted to know as much as he could about where he was before he did. He hoped Artimus wouldn't be going to too much trouble. Artimus had assured Jeff that the task wouldn't be difficult, but Jeff worried he might have been being polite.

Baldwin turned the lights off. Jeff's eyes were open, and he was staring at the ceiling. He was absolutely *exhausted*, but he didn't want to have the dreams again – particularly not now that he knew a 'pheerion' was a real thing.

He looked at the clock. It said 8.85. So *they don't use the same clocks as us. Base 10?* Jeff wondered. A base 10 system would make a lot more sense than what Jeff was used to. Jeff's father had told him stories that even when he was a kid they had talked about switching to metric, but it never really got going. Since Jeff's father was a scientist, he often used metric units.

Jeff watched the clock switch over to 8.86, then, after a while, 8.87. Jeff decided to try to count it out and when it switched to 8.88, Jeff started counting: "One thousand 1, one thousand 2, one thousand 3..."

By the time it switched to 8.89, Jeff had just hit "One thousand 92".

So he guessed there were about 90 seconds in one of their minutes. Since he was guessing they used a base 10 time system, he assumed there would be about 9000 earth seconds in one of their hours.

So 9000 Earth seconds would be 2.5 hours meaning each of their hours would be 2.5 Earth hours. Again assuming a base 10 system, that would make a 10 hour day here equal to a 25 hour day on Earth.

Jeff was pleased with himself for thinking that through, but then he could hear his father's voice in his head: "So you made a rough estimate followed by some guesses and assumptions and then used math to try to give your guesses and assumptions some credibility? You could have just as easily guessed the whole thing and been as accurate."

Oh well. At least it had kept him awake another 10 minutes... or 6.67 minutes.

Jeff laughed at his own geekiness.

His eyes drifted shut, then snapped open again. Within a few more minutes, they were drifting closed again, and Jeff was too tired to resist.

After stretches of talking pumpkins and dancing elephants, the creature appeared.

Jeff didn't wake as he normally did but had a few moments to observe the creature.

It looked exactly like the image Baldwin had showed him. It was a lizard, a little larger than a man, but it stood upright. It had the snout of a lizard, but it seemed a bit less pronounced and more expressive than an actual lizard face.

Its clothing appeared to be a type of leather that covered its torso and upper legs. It appeared military – vaguely similar to a Roman centurion's uniform with a sword hanging from a belt.

And this time it did something Jeff had either never noticed before or didn't remember.

It spoke.

It was speaking in a croaking, wheezing voice in a language Jeff couldn't understand.

Jeff's heart was pounding so loudly he could hear the thumping. He tried to run, tried to get away, but he was paralyzed.

While Jeff couldn't understand the meaning of the words, he did have a clear sense that the words were challenging – threatening. The pheerion raised its hand as if to strike.

Jeff's eyes snapped open.

Chapter 19:

Jeff leaned back, closed his eyes and soaked in the feeling of warm sunshine on his face.

He hadn't gotten much sleep after the nightmare.

When morning finally came, Baldwin leant him some clothes, and the two of them walked to a nearby park.

Jeff was beginning to feel relaxed for the first time since he had been there. He watched the neighborhood kids run and play. There was an area that was immediately recognizable as a playground even though the equipment was unique.

There were some 'swings', but they weren't hanging from chains. They were hanging from thick, elastic bands, and they could bounce up and down as well as swing back and forth. Some parents were bouncing young children in them without swinging them at all.

Some kids were climbing a jungle gym that had a strange design but otherwise wasn't that different from those on which Jeff had played when he was younger.

Jeff's favorite piece – and one he was hoping to try when he got a chance – was a small 'roller-coaster' or at least something very similar to what Jeff knew as a roller-coaster. It only had one car with seats for six kids. It wasn't powered, but the kids could push it up the hill from a ramp that ran along-side. At the top of the hill, they locked it in place, climbed in and then let it go. It ran, reasonably fast, around a winding track before eventually coming to a stop back at the bottom of the hill – all the while making a satisfying 'clackity-clack' sound that brought back childhood memories of good times for Jeff.

Damn. I've got to try that.

The ground around all of the playground equipment was padded with a thick, spongy rubber foam.

"You can go ahead and hang out with your friends,"

Jeff said to Baldwin. "Don't feel like you have to babysit me. I'm good just sitting here enjoying the sunshine."

Baldwin looked around. "I'm okay."

Jeff had the feeling that Baldwin was kind of shy. Artimus and Nahima both seemed very outgoing, but Jeff sensed that Baldwin felt a little out of place even with his own family. Jeff wondered what their mother had been like, but he didn't want to ask. There were a number of photos of her around the house, and based on Nahima and Baldwin's apparent ages in the photos, Jeff thought that she had probably died relatively recently.

"What does your father do?" Jeff asked.

"You mean for a job?"

"Yeah, I'm just sort of curious. He seems like an interesting guy."

"He's a Bishop... and he's on the governing council."

Jeff looked at him in surprise. "Bishop? Like with the church?"

"Sure." Baldwin shrugged. "What other kind of Bishop is there?"

"That's cool... I never would have guessed it though."

"Cool?" Baldwin looked at him with a puzzled expression.

Damn!

Jeff cringed. He had thought there must be words or phrases that they wouldn't recognize here – he had heard Baldwin and Nahima use words and phrases he didn't know – but he had been careful and so far hadn't got caught using anything unfamiliar.

"Uh, I mean good. When do you have to go back to school?" He changed the subject abruptly.

"We don't have to go this whole week. Every two months, we get a week off." Baldwin had picked up the habit of explaining things in great detail to Jeff.

Jeff wondered to himself what 'weeks' and 'months' were, but he kept his question to himself and assumed they were similar to what he knew.

Jeff saw an ant crawling toward his foot. As he got a better look, he realized it wasn't actually an ant. It was similar but had four – rather than three – body segments and two sets of legs on each of the middle two body sections for a total of eight legs rather than six.

His foot hovered over the 'ant' and as the shadow passed over the bug, it stopped, and as it stopped, Jeff sensed a twinge. Jeff couldn't relate the feeling to anything he had ever felt before, but there was just sort of a 'tickle' in the back of his brain at the moment the ant stopped.

He had the brief – *crazy* – idea that he had some mental connection with the ant. He imagined the ant turning to the left... and...

The ant did start moving to the left!

Then Jeff imagined it moving the other way...

And...

It continued going the way it had been going.

But then...

It stopped and turned the direction Jeff had been imagining!

Wild! Jeff thought to himself. He glanced at Baldwin who didn't seem to be paying any attention.

He looked back at the ant, and *willed* it to do a back flip.

...

...

...

It didn't.

It pretty much just kept walking the way it had been.

Jeff leaned back and smiled at his own silliness.

"Uh oh," Baldwin tensed noticeably.

"What's wrong?" Jeff asked.

"Here comes Magnus Duanan. He's such a jerk... the one with the blue shirt."

Jeff glanced in the direction Baldwin was indicating with his eyes. He saw two big kids, probably about his age. They were walking and tossing a glowing blue ball back and forth. The ball looked like it was made from some sort of energy field, and they were each wearing special gloves.

"Do you want to go?" Jeff asked.

Baldwin shook his head. "I wouldn't want to give him the satisfaction."

Jeff saw Magnus say something to his friend, and then he pointed in their direction.

Jeff had a bad feeling.

It seemed that jerks were an unfortunate, universal fact of life. The same little voice that told Jeff he could trust Baldwin and his family was telling him just the opposite about those two.

The thuglings worked their way casually toward Jeff and Baldwin. They continued throwing the ball as if they were just playing catch, but Jeff was sure they were intentionally trying to get closer to Baldwin.

"Hey, there's Winfred," Magnus said as if he had just noticed him. He was intentionally speaking loudly enough that Jeff and Baldwin could hear him as he continued to casually toss the ball. He had an expression – an almost comically exaggerated leer – that Jeff might have found amusing, if it wasn't being worn by someone who might be kicking his ass in the next few moments.

"I'm surprised he's not helping his father on some project to help Doclotnurians wipe their back-ends or something."

Baldwin tensed. Jeff could see the anger rising in his face, but he clearly wouldn't have a chance against those two goons if things got physical.

Jeff was getting nervous himself.

Even though he didn't know the thugs, he knew their type. They were the type who could look at a nest of freshly hatched birds, see their beaks open and close as they teetered awkwardly – spreading their wings for the first time – and think: 'I wonder what kind of sound it would make if I hit them with a rock?'

"Hey Winfred! Why don't you go live in Doclotnury if you like them so much?"

Jeff could see the internal battle Baldwin was fighting. Part of him wanted to go punch Magnus, but he was being held back by the part of him that didn't want to get pummeled into a mushy, bloody mess.

"Yeah," the other goon joined in. He was tucking his special glove into his belt – apparently getting ready in case Baldwin decided to play. "Why don't you move to Doclotnury if you like it so much?"

"Your father could probably get a job cleaning toilets or something," Magnus added.

That insult did it.

Baldwin's brain was no longer in charge, and he jumped up. Jeff grabbed his arm, but he jerked it away. He charged toward Magnus, but before he could get to him, Magnus' friend – Goon 2 – got him from the side.

Goon 2 put Baldwin in a head-lock. Baldwin struggled, but he was no match for the larger, stronger boy. He squirmed and twisted, but the other boy's grip just got tighter. Baldwin's feet were kicking – at times both feet lifted off the ground simultaneously leaving him dangling by his neck. A few curious onlookers began to gawk, but Jeff didn't see any adults or anyone else who seemed willing to get involved.

Jeff saw Magnus grinning, and he got a sick feeling in his stomach. When it was clear Magnus intended to punch the captive Baldwin, Jeff got to his feet. "NO!!"

The three looked at Jeff.

Magnus turned to face him.

Be confident, be confident, be confident, Jeff told himself. He looked Magnus right in the eye. But the sharp angle at which he had to tilt his head to accomplish that wasn't making him nearly as confident as he was hoping to be.

Magnus grinned – a stupid, toothy grin. The two faced each other for what seemed a very long time, but Jeff had found his perception of time was often skewed in situations like that. Out of the corners of his eyes, Jeff could see a small crowd gathering.

Without any warning, Magnus punched, but *somehow* Jeff saw it coming. He was so focused, that it almost seemed like the thug was moving in slow motion. He caught Magnus' right hand with his left, and for a brief moment, the two of them looked down at the joined hands in equal surprise.

Then Jeff *threw* the hand down with as much force as he could manage, and Magnus teetered off balance for a moment. As he teetered, Jeff grabbed two solid handfuls of Magnus' shirt. He jerked Magnus toward him, and then pushed him back just as quickly, releasing his hold on the shirt at just the right moment to send Magnus flying.

Magnus went back so fast that his butt was leading the way, and he had had no hope of getting his feet under him. He stumbled and fell hard on his ass about ten feet from Jeff.

For a brief moment, Jeff felt 100 eyes on him, then he put his attention back to the only two that really mattered at the moment. Magnus looked at him from the ground with a mix of what looked like surprise and, amazingly, *fear.*

Magnus got shakily to his feet, keeping his eyes on Jeff but not getting any closer. He glanced at his friend who dropped his hold on Baldwin as if by wordless command, and the two of them walked away – calmly but awkwardly.

Baldwin looked at Jeff with an expression of complete gratitude and awe. "Wow! How'd you do that?"

Jeff looked at his hands. "I don't know. I guess it was adrenaline... maybe I took him by surprise... plus a lot of luck."

"Let's just try to avoid any more adventures today." He smiled. "I don't think we could get that lucky twice in the same day."

Chapter 20:

Jeff decided it was time to come clean.

He fidgeted nervously and pushed his food around on his plate.

He felt he could trust them. He wasn't sure what would happen after he told them who he was, but if all well, he was hoping they could help him find his father.

Artimus Winfred – though Jeff never would have guessed based on his home-life – was a very important person in that strange world.

The thing that seemed most difficult to Jeff was the act of raising the subject. He had been lying for the past day, and it was a little awkward to admit his deception to the family who had been so kind to him.

He tried to make eye contact with Artimus, but it seemed that every time he tried, Artimus was looking somewhere else.

Jeff fumbled with a bowl and nearly dropped it. He was tense and nervous and his hands felt shaky.

Again he looked at Artimus and this time Artimus met his gaze. Artimus' eyebrows lifted inquisitively.

And... Jeff quickly looked down at his plate.

There were several more minutes of awkward silence and then Artimus spoke: "So, Jeff, I ran your retina through the computer, and it didn't match anyone."

Artimus paused, took a bite of food and allowed that to sink in.

The perfect opening, Jeff thought. He opened his mouth to speak.

And nothing came out.

Artimus continued: "Now, as you may know, we have pretty good record keeping, and everyone who is born is registered, so it's very unusual that you wouldn't come up."

His face turned a bit more serious than Jeff had seen up to that point. He looked Jeff directly in the eye. "I don't want to accuse you of anything, but is it possible you know more than you're telling us?"

Jeff was nearly quivering, but he just couldn't find the words. He tried to imagine how to even begin to explain.

Artimus continued, this time in a slightly quieter, subdued voice: "If you're a Doclotnurian, you should know you're among friends." His face became inquisitive, almost hopeful.

Jeff's face flushed. He decided to just get his mouth moving and see what came out. "Ummmm... I'm really sorry, but I haven't been telling the complete truth. I didn't really want to deceive you... it's just... I didn't think you'd believe me."

He looked around the table at all three faces. He felt terribly guilty but also very relieved that he had gotten past the part he had been most dreading. He would, hopefully, soon be completely unburdened.

The table was absolutely silent. The three were listening intently to every word, and now that Jeff had gotten that far, he ran into another mental wall. How could he explain it?

"Uhhhh... this is going to sound crazy." As Jeff imagined his next words, they really did seem crazy. *Will they buy this at all?*

"I... uh... I... I'm not from here... I'm from a different place." Jeff decided that a phrase like 'alternate dimension' might lose them. He decided to start from the beginning and ease into it.

"My father was a scientist, and he... 'disappeared'... about a year ago. The police assumed he had met with foul play and was probably dead." Jeff was getting a little choked up. "I never believed that. I knew I was probably thinking with my heart instead of my head, but I felt like he was still alive... *somewhere*."

The three were listening to him intently. He almost

wished someone would jump in with a question or some other interruption. He could feel his mouth going dry, and he was starting to feel very uncomfortable being the complete center of attention.

"Anyway, yesterday I was in his office, and I found this really weird... *thing*. It had an opening that seemed to..." He paused before deciding to just charge ahead. "It seemed to lead to another world."

He paused again to read the faces of his audience. They were paying absolute attention to him, but he couldn't tell if they believed him or not. There were no expressions of either shock or disbelief at his last pronouncement, but he couldn't tell if that meant they did believe him or just thought it was so stupid it didn't even justify a response.

"I dropped a rope through that... *portal*... and climbed down.   It was... like a hole in the sky... over the forest. That's how I ended up there."

Well, that was it.

Jeff had said it.

He couldn't tell if his hosts believed him or not. They seemed to be at least considering it. The four of them sat in silence for a few moments, and the longer the silence went, the more uncomfortable Jeff became.

Finally, Artimus broke the silence: "So why did you tell us you couldn't remember anything?"

"I'm REALLY sorry about that. I just thought it would be best... until I knew more about this place. I didn't think anybody would believe me if I told the truth."

Artimus nodded. He seemed to believe him.

There was another long, silent moment.

"So, you're looking for your father," Artimus said. "Is there any way we can help you? What's his name?"

Jeff felt a huge sense of relief wash over him. It seemed Artimus believed him. "His name is Jeffrey Browning... *Dr.* Jeffrey Browning."

Artimus seemed to be thinking. "Hmmm, I don't

know anybody who goes by that name, but that gives us something to start with. I can run that through the computer. I certainly haven't heard of anybody falling out of the sky." He thought a bit longer but seemed to be drawing a blank. "Do you have any photos?"

Jeff shook his head. He never carried photos... *Wait!*

Jeff remembered the locket and fished around in his shirt. As he pulled it out, he saw Artimus' fork stop in mid-air. His eyes shot to the locket, and his mouth hung open in what Jeff interpreted as a shocked gape that lasted a second or two. Artimus looked pointedly at Nahima who seemed confused, and then Artimus' eyes went back to the locket.

Jeff pulled the chain over his head, opened the locket and held it out to Artimus, but Artimus didn't reach for it.

Jeff began to get a little nervous. Artimus seemed to be acting very strangely. He was staring fixatedly at the locket but not moving. Finally, after ten seconds, he began to reach, slowly, *slowly* for the locket. Jeff thought it looked like his hand was trembling.

As he touched the locket, he looked at Nahima again, but she didn't seem to know what to do or say.

Artimus held the locket, but kept it at arm's length. He looked at the photo of Jeff's father then up at Jeff, then back to the photo. His face was very hard to read. He seemed nervous, or... *something.*

"If you'll excuse me," Artimus said somewhat abruptly. "I need to talk to Nahima for a moment."

He got up and walked briskly out of the room with Nahima close behind.

Baldwin shrugged and went back to his food.

From the other room, Jeff could hear the conversation. They seemed to be talking in forceful whispers, but the acoustics and volume of their speaking carried their voices clearly into the kitchen.

"What's going on? Did someone put him up to this?" Artimus asked.

"I don't know." Nahima responded

"Who would do something like this? Is Jeff part of it, or is someone just using him?"

Jeff flushed. "This is a little embarrassing."

Baldwin's cheeks were stuffed with food. He looked at Jeff silently but quizzically. He gulped heavily and said: "What are you talking about?"

"Them." He looked in the direction of Artimus and Nahima's voices. "The way they're talking about me."

Baldwin still seemed confused. "Why do you think they're talking about you?"

"Well their voices are carrying fairly clearly."

Baldwin gave him a strange look. "I can't hear anything."

He shrugged and went back to his food.

"Do you think he's just a con-artist?" Artimus asked. "Maybe it's just a scam to get some money."

"Dad," Nahima said. "I trust him."

There was a long, silent moment before Artimus responded.

"You do?"

"Yes Dad, I do."

"Well you know that means a lot to me."

"I feel fairly strongly about it."

There was another long pause before Artimus spoke again. "Well that changes things... I'm still skeptical, but maybe I should give him a chance."

Chapter 21:

It took several minutes after the conversation before Artimus and Nahima came back. Jeff was getting more and more nervous. It was clear that they had doubts about his story, but he wasn't supposed to know that. *Am I?* As far as he knew, they thought their conversation was private. Baldwin didn't seem to hear it. *Maybe it's just something about where I'm sitting.*

Artimus and Nahima took their seats, and Jeff noticed Artimus was holding Jeff's baseball bat.

"I'm sorry," Artimus said with a forced smile as he took his seat. He ate a couple bites and tried to act casual, but he was clearly not as calm as he tried to appear. "Tell me Jeff," he said as he reached down and lifted the bat. "What is this?"

Jeff realized it was a test, and he took the bat from Artimus. "This? This is a baseball bat."

Artimus nodded and looked intently at Jeff. "Tell me about... baseball."

"Well, sometime in the 1800's... in my world, we are in the year 2008 now, so we're talking about maybe 150 years ago. I'm not clear on the details... but anyway in the 1800's a guy named Abner Doubleday, created a game called baseball. I don't know as much as I should about the origins, and there may have been more people involved... but he seems to get the credit.

"To play, you have a large field called a baseball diamond. It's called a diamond because the bases are laid out in a diamond." Jeff used his hands to show the approximate lay-out of a baseball field as he spoke. "There are four bases... if you count home plate. The bases are ninety feet apart. Home plate is here, at the point of the diamond, and the foul lines run out through first and third bases here and here. Second base is between first and third bases here. The area defined by the bases is called the 'infield', this area out here." He swept his hand across his imaginary outfield. "Is the 'outfield'. You have four 'infielders' – first baseman, second baseman, shortstop and third baseman. In the outfield you have a right fielder, center fielder and left fielder.

"The pitcher is on the pitcher's mound, here, in the center of the diamond, and then you have the catcher behind home-plate."

Jeff looked up for a moment to read faces. He was sure none of them were really following what he was saying, but they were paying attention.

"The visiting team bats first, so the home-team is in the field to start the game. When they get to the bottom of the inning, they'll switch places and all the people who were in the field will come in to bat... of course in the American League they'll have a designated hitter bat for the pitcher... I never was a fan of that, but what are you going to do?

"The pitcher has a small, white ball with red stitching about this big." Jeff illustrated the size of a baseball. "He throws it and tries to get it past the batter who waits and swings one of these baseball bats and tries to hit the ball." Jeff lifted the bat to illustrate and then decided to take it a step farther. He stood up, got a good grip on the bat, took a batting stance, and after making sure he had plenty of room, began taking some practice swings.

"Now you have to imagine home-plate here," he said as he traced an outline of home-plate on the floor with the bat. "Because that defines the strike zone. The strike zone is an imaginary window that's as wide as the plate and between the batter's shoulder and knees." He waved his hand back and forth and up and down to show the approximate location of the strike zone. "There's an umpire behind the catcher to call balls and strikes.

"So the pitcher throws the ball." Jeff put the bat on his shoulder and pointed to an imaginary pitcher. "And if the batter doesn't swing, it's either a ball or strike depending on if it's in or out of the strike zone. Three strikes and the batter is 'out', four balls is a 'walk', and the batter gets to go to first base. Three outs, and the offensive team goes back on defense. One 'inning' is a set in which both teams have played offense and defense. Nine innings make up the whole game... unless the ninth inning ends in a tie, and then it goes into extra innings... oh, and if the home team is leading after eight and a half innings, they don't play the last half of the ninth inning.

"Now if the batter does swing and misses the ball," Jeff swung his bat to illustrate. "It's a strike even if it's out of the strike zone. If the ball goes 'foul' – outside the foul lines..." Jeff gestured in the direction of imaginary foul lines. "It counts as a strike... unless there are already two strikes, because the at-bat can't end on a foul... unless a player catches it..."

Artimus was starting to laugh, and once he started, Nahima and Baldwin joined in until the three of them were laughing uncontrollably. It was contagious and Jeff found himself laughing too.

"Okay," Artimus said. "If you can make all that up, you deserve anything you can con out of me." He put his hand on Jeff's shoulder.

Then things got weird.

Artimus put his arms around Jeff and pulled him in for a long hug.

Jeff wasn't sure if he was supposed to hug back, so his arms moved up and down trying to decide where to go.

"I hope we can find your father."

Jeff thought it almost looked like Artimus was going to cry.

Chapter 22:

Jeff stared at the ceiling. He laughed to himself at Baldwin's snoring.

Artimus wanted Jeff to come to the Governing Council the next day. He told Jeff there were important things going on and – for some reason – Artimus thought Jeff might be able to help. He told Jeff he'd tell him more the next day, but he thought it might, indirectly, help Jeff find his father.

The whole idea that Artimus seemed to want something from him but wouldn't tell him much about what it was – though it clearly seemed important to him – had Jeff very uptight.

There were other things weighing on his mind as well.

As usual, he didn't want the nightmares. There was something about that creature that affected him emotionally far more than was rational.

It struck a chord of primal fear within Jeff.

In addition to those concerns, he had realized this was the second night he wouldn't be home. Jeff was energized by the thought that his father might be alive and somewhere relatively nearby – though Jeff tried to avoid being irrationally optimistic. The hope made him feel *alive* in a way that he hadn't felt since his father had disappeared. That optimism combined with the sheer wonder of the unique, fresh place had ended the bored depression Jeff had been stuck in two days before.

But what about my mother? She has to be worried sick, and now she is...

Alone.

The emotion nearly overwhelmed Jeff as he lay there in the dark. He felt his throat tightening as he pictured his mom sitting alone in their big, cold house.

Could she have figured out what happened? Jeff leaned over and opened a drawer in a nightstand by his bed. His father's keys were in the pocket of the Jeans he had worn yesterday. He pulled the keys out and looked at them.

They were the only clue. He had locked the office door and turned off the light, so the only thing out of place would be the missing keys. He wondered if his mother could figure it out from that.

No.

How could she?

It was just a missing set of keys. What would tie them to the office? If anything, she'd assume he had run away and taken the keys as a reminder of his father.

It's probably best if she doesn't figure it out, Jeff rationalized. *If she figured it out, she probably wouldn't just enter the portal... she'd tell someone.*

Once other people knew about the portal, what would/will happen? Will they send soldiers in? Will it be the start of an inter-dimensional war?

Jeff tried not to think about it. *Think happy thoughts,* he told himself.

He imagined meeting up with his father again, but that just seemed impossible.

As much as he rationalized and hoped his father might be here, the idea of actually finding him just didn't seem like a realistic possibility.

If he came down at the same place I did, he might have run into one of those snakes...

There I go again.

Jeff exhaled loudly. He needed to clear his mind –. needed to relax and stop over-thinking everything.

Needed to get some sleep...

But then will I dream about the pheerion?

Jeff twisted the pillow around his head and squeezed. "Aaaaarrrrgh"

His brain went around in those circles until it finally just wore itself out.

He could see a figure in the distance...

It was moving toward him, it had an unusual gate.

As it got closer, he began to recognize a shape.

It looked like a rabbit.

Not a normal rabbit, more like a human sized rabbit hopping upright. Like the Easter Bunny.

But it wasn't a man wearing an Easter Bunny suit. The huge hind legs had mass and sinew, like a *real* Easter Bunny, not a costume.

As it got closer, he saw that it had a man's face.

Not just any man.

It looked like Richard Nixon.

Nixon turned toward him and said: "What are you looking at... freak."

Chapter 23:

Jeff's eyes ran across the rough, scaly skin. He tried to avoid looking directly into the red, piercing eyes, but he knew he couldn't avoid it.

He was always drawn to the red eyes, and when he met them, he knew he would recognize the pure evil behind them.

An evil that would chill his soul.

His eyes locked onto the red eyes, and everything else in his peripheral vision distorted and faded.

All he could see were eyes and flashing teeth as the creature spoke in its harsh, wheezing, croaking voice.

As it spoke – in the same unrecognizable language Jeff had heard the night before – Jeff could understand what it was saying. He still heard the foreign words, and he didn't really understand them, but it was almost as if a voice in the back of his head translated as the creature spoke: "You can't stop me, boy..."

Jeff's eyes flashed open, and he was back in Baldwin's room. Baldwin's snoring was comforting, albeit window rattling.

Jeff looked the clock: 1:82

Jeff had learned that they were indeed on a ten hour day as he had guessed, and that would make it somewhere between the equivalent of 4 and 5 am. Jeff didn't feel up to doing the rest of the math.

Well, I guess it's late enough I can just get up.

He picked up the 'dress clothes' that Baldwin and Artimus had given him the night before for his big day and, as quietly as possible, went to the bathroom to shower.

When he had finished his shower, he got to use one of the niftier gadgets Baldwin had shown him. There was a small, metal plate built into the shower stall wall, and after Jeff turned off the water, he touched the panel with an index finger.

The stall was washed with a soft, warm light, and over a period of about five seconds, all the water droplets on Jeff's body and also the shower surfaces vanished. His hair was still somewhat wet but drier than it normally would have been coming right out of the shower. He stepped out of the stall, grabbed the shirt and pants and pulled them on.

They didn't seem much different than the casual, comfortable clothes that he had worn yesterday. They did seem similar to what Artimus had been wearing when he returned from work, but Jeff wasn't really sure what made them 'dress'.

Jeff made his way to the kitchen and was a little surprised to find Artimus already there and dressed.

"Good morning," Artimus said brightly and rose from his seat. "Can I get you anything to eat?"

"Sure, thanks. Anything is fine. Don't go to any trouble."

While Jeff generally found the food absolutely delicious, he thought the breakfast foods were bland and uninspiring. They didn't seem to offer nearly as much fat or sugar as he typically had for breakfast.

"Now first off," Artimus said. "I should tell you, don't be nervous. I don't expect you to really do anything today. I just want you to listen and learn. If, after getting a feel for what's going on, you have any thoughts or comments, please share anything that comes to mind."

Jeff nodded.

Artimus put a plate in front of Jeff with a yellowish square of some sort of dry, crumbly food and placed a glass of juice beside that. Artimus took a plate and glass for himself and sat down. He had a bite and then continued.

"I think Baldwin told you a little bit about our history."

Jeff nodded again and took a bite from his breakfast. It had the consistency of cornbread but with an unusual taste that Jeff couldn't identify. It wasn't bad but nothing special either.

"As, I think you know, our ancestors came from Doclotnury originally, and we lived under their authority up until about twenty-five years ago. At that time, we fought a war for the right to govern ourselves."

Artimus exhaled loudly and took a sip of fruit juice. It seemed that he was uncomfortable about what he was about to say. "Since that war, people here have not gotten past their hostility and distrust with Doclotnury."

He paused again and took a bite of food. Jeff sensed that Artimus felt his words were important, and he wanted to make sure that he expressed himself clearly.

"I feel... very strongly... that we need to re-establish ties with our Doclotnurian brothers. Humans are the most technologically advanced species on this planet. We don't have a large population, and we are very limited in terms of where we can live, what resources we can access, etcetera. I don't think it's right... or smart, to remain estranged from the only other humans on the planet."

"If your war was only twenty-five years ago, and prior to that you were governed by them, you must still have friends, relatives and other close ties with Doclotnury," Jeff commented.

Artimus nodded. "Yes... yes, we do. But twenty-five years also is not a lot of time to heal from some deep wounds of a violent, bloody war." He glanced down at his forearm, and Jeff's eyes went there too. There was a large scar that Jeff had noticed earlier. Artimus pulled his sleeve over it before taking another bite of food.

"There are a lot of... VERY... conflicted emotions regarding all this.

"Now this might seem like I'm going off on a tangent, but I'll try to explain why I think it all ties together in a minute. We've been having a terrible drought recently.

You may have noticed the arid area between the forest and Caesurmia."

Jeff nodded.

"That area used to be lush with streams and vegetation, but it's been drying up for the past year. We still manage, but resources are becoming scarcer. It's getting harder to live the comfortable lives to which we've become accustomed."

He paused again to have a few bites and sip some juice. Jeff also took the opportunity to have some of his own.

"Now the reason I mentioned it and feel it's related to some of the other problems we're having is: Those limited resources are causing stress. If we had everything we wanted, I think people would be more willing to make efforts to improve our relationship with Doclotnury. While it doesn't make any logical sense, some people try to point to Doclotnury as some sort of explanation for why we're having problems. It's easier to blame and distrust them than it is to face the fact that we're having problems that are beyond anybody's control."

Artimus had finished his breakfast, and he pushed the plate aside. "Are you following me so far?"

Jeff nodded. It seemed that Artimus had a very clear, direct way of communicating, and Jeff had no problem understanding him.

"Now, with that background out of the way, we can get to the real problem. You've heard of the pheerions?"

Jeff's stomach tensed as he thought of the creature in his dreams. He nodded slowly.

"The pheerions have been threatening war with Doclotnury. There's a general – General Rasp – who has an armada of ships that appear to be headed for war with Doclotnury. The pheerions don't have the technology we have, but they're fierce and have large numbers.

"We have to help the Doclotnurians, or I fear, they'll be over-run. I have been arguing for weeks that we need to help, but I'm afraid I'm still in the minority."

Jeff thought about the creature from his dreams, and the thought of fighting an army of them seemed terrifying. "Why won't they help? Once the pheerions defeat Doclotnury, will they stop? Isn't there a chance they'll come here?"

"I'm glad you get it, though I guess I should have assumed you would. Those are my thoughts exactly. I don't know if we even have a choice. We *must* fight the pheerions now, before they get a foothold on this continent."

"But... can't people understand that? Is it really that they don't like the Doclotnurians, or is it something else? Are they afraid?"

"I think you have it now. We've become very... *comfortable*... here. We have a safe, orderly society. I think that's a big reason people don't want to get involved... *fear*... but it's easier to say: 'I don't want to help because I don't care about those bastards' than it is to say: 'I don't want to help because I'm afraid.'

"And when they're not admitting their real motivations for their actions, it's hard to reason with them."

Jeff found himself getting almost... angry. "But they've got to understand, they've got to make a stand, this is too important."

Artimus smiled again. "We can't really fault people, too much, for being weak, short-sighted and selfish. Those characteristics don't make them terrible... those characteristics just make them... people.

"But that doesn't mean we can't strive for something better."

Chapter 24:

Jeff admired the sleek lines of Artimus' car before they got in. He caught a slight smile from Artimus and guessed that he took some pride in his car. It was very different from the one Nahima had been driving – larger, more muscular and much more elaborately styled.

The materials and build quality of Artimus' car were clearly superior to those of the one Nahima had been driving. The differences seemed similar to those of a $70,000 sport sedan back home compared to a $15,000 econo-box.

As they approached, the two front doors opened.

Hmmmm, did Artimus push something or are there some sort of sensors? Jeff was curious but didn't actually ask. He had felt very foolish since arriving, and he was doing his best to casually deal with each new thing he saw. He felt self-conscious and out of place but was doing his best to blend... *What's that? A two-headed, web-footed purple giraffe with a seven-foot long, two-pronged penis *Yawn* whatever.*

Jeff climbed in and sank into the perfectly formed seat. Again, he thought he caught a smile from Artimus. It was more comfortable than the couch that had so impressed Jeff two days before.

Artimus hit a button on the dashboard, and the craft came to life with a rhythmic hum. Lights from instrument panels illuminated Artimus' face as he quickly and absentmindedly began working controls. The roof of the vehicle slid back, and the side windows dropped into the doors leaving the cockpit open.

The garage door behind them opened, and the car lifted gently. Jeff squinted uncomfortably. The bright morning sunshine hurt his eyes as they backed out of the dimly lit garage. The moment the front end had cleared the doorway, Artimus twisted the yoke, and they did a quick, perfect 180. Artimus tilted the nose upward, pulled a lever and they accelerated forcefully at a forty-five degree angle with the horizon.

They continued to accelerate, and Artimus twisted the nose up until they were climbing... *vertically*. Artimus yanked back the accelerator, and Jeff felt his seat depress several inches as they rocketed straight up at an amazing rate. Jeff had to struggle to pull air into his lungs, and he tried to move his arms but couldn't. He glanced at Artimus and saw he had a huge grin.

He's showing off.

After about ten seconds they slowed. Artimus leveled the vehicle and brought it to a near complete stop. From there, Jeff could see the city spread out below them.

"Technically speaking, this isn't completely legal... but I know some people." Artimus looked at Jeff and winked with the grin still plastered to his face.

If Jeff had known, a few minutes prior, that they were going to climb to that dizzying height in the open vehicle, he would have been nervous and reluctant, but it happened so fast he didn't have time to be scared. The view was so spectacular and the feeling of floating there so peaceful that he just soaked it in.

After a minute or two of just hanging there, Artimus pointed the nose down and began to descend at a much more leisurely pace than he had used to climb.

As they picked up a little speed, he did some barrel rolls, and again, Jeff didn't really have time to be scared until he was already into it. They descended for a few minutes until they were within a few hundred feet of what appeared to be a random mess of flying cars weaving in and out of streams of traffic.

Artimus hit a button and took his hands off the controls. "Auto-pilot," he explained. "All mobiles are required to use it within the city limits. It looks like a mess, but all the mobiles can communicate with one-another. There's no chance of contact."

Jeff was mesmerized by the computer controlled and choreographed dance of the flying cars. There were streams of cars criss-crossing above and below them. Occasionally a car would leave one stream and join another.

Artimus' car veered out of their stream and took a line away from everybody else. Jeff grabbed his armrests as he saw they were headed directly toward a building. He opened his mouth to shout a warning, but before he could form any words, a door opened in front of them, and they settled into a small garage.

The vehicle doors opened. Artimus hopped out of the car and stretched.

Jeff felt a little shaky and sat for a few moments, trying to collect himself, before getting out. When he was ready, he exited slowly. The garage door was still open behind them, and Jeff went to check out the view.

They were about twenty stories up, and Jeff had a nice overview of the streets below. The general sights and activities were similar to what Jeff would expect in any city, but it looked and *smelled* much cleaner than the cities with which Jeff was familiar.

It was a spectacular sight.

Artimus, after collecting a few things from the car, joined Jeff and stood silently beside him, patiently giving him all the time he wanted to take in the sights. When Jeff was done, Artimus directed him to a door that led into a large office. It was elaborately decorated, lavishly furnished, and it had an enormous window that looked out over the city. Jeff walked to the window and again admired the view.

Artimus looked through some things on his desk and then said: "Codi?"

"Good morning Father Winfred," a voice said.

"Good morning."

Jeff found it odd that he would say good morning to, what Jeff assumed was a computer.

"Would you please contact Alvina and Goldwin and ask them if they could stop by before session?"

"Certainly Father."

Artimus walked over next to Jeff and looked out the window. They both stood there silently for several minutes before Artimus finally spoke.

"You know, I don't do this often enough... just observe. There's so much to see, isn't there? So much going on that just blends into the background after a while."

They stood in silence for several more minutes.

"You sometimes forget," Artimus said, "all those people... they have thoughts and dreams and lives and families. If you sat down with any one of them, they'd have so many stories to tell – things they've done, things they wished they had done, things they're looking forward to."

Jeff turned to look at him. He saw character in Artimus' face that he had never really noticed before. There was a strength and dignity... yet slight hints of weakness and uncertainty. For a brief moment, Jeff thought he recognized all of humanity in that one face.

Artimus turned to face Jeff. "Tell me about your father," he said with a smile.

"Uhhh, well..."

Back home, it seemed that everyone already knew Jeff's father. He realized at that moment that he had never even tried to describe or explain him to anybody who had no idea who he was.

"He's a very smart man... *very* smart. He's probably one of the smartest people in the world."

As soon as Jeff said that, he began to blush.

"And I'm not just saying that like every kid thinks his father is the smartest guy in the world... I've actually heard other people describe him that way. He's a great physicist... one of the best. He's a professor at one of the most prestigious universities in my country... in fact one person who is viewed by many people as *the* smartest person... ever... worked at that same university seventy years ago."

"Is he a good man, a thoughtful man, a kind man?" Artimus asked.

"Yes. I'd say so." Jeff blushed again. "Of course I'm probably prejudiced, but I've always found him to be giving... patient... sometimes I feel a little..."

"What?" Artimus asked and turned to look at him.

"I guess sometimes I feel like I'll never be as good as him."

"Well... I think everyone... at some time or another... wonders if they'll ever be able to do the things they see other people doing. And then one day, they realize they're simply doing them."

"Father," The computer's voice spoke again, but then Jeff realized it was an actual person who had entered the room.

"I'm sorry. I didn't realize you had someone in here," the young woman said.

"No, please, come in. I have someone I'd like you to meet. Jeff this is my assistant Codi. Codi, this is Jeff. He's a very special young man."

She shook Jeff's hand, then turned to Artimus. "I just wanted to tell you that Councilwoman Royer is here."

"Please send her in."

A neatly dressed woman in her fifties entered and smiled at Artimus. Following closely behind her was a man about Artimus' age who also had a very professional look about him.

"Alvina and Goldwin, good, you're both here." Artimus walked over, shook both their hands and kissed Alvina on the cheek. Then he stretched his arm out behind them and swept them around, directing them toward Jeff. "There's someone I want you to meet. This is Jeff. He's a very special young man. Jeff, this is councilwoman Royer."

Jeff shook her hand.

"And councilman Bellows."

Jeff shook his hand.

"If neither of you mind, I'd like Jeff to sit in with us. I can't really explain everything right now, but I think Jeff may be able to offer us some help."

Jeff was getting uncomfortable with the idea that Artimus seemed to think he could 'help'. Jeff realized that he may have a unique perspective from living in a different society, but he wasn't a great student of history or people. He wasn't sure how living somewhere else gave him any special qualification to help with governmental matters of the highest importance – *matters of war.*

Jeff was hoping that Artimus didn't expect him to directly participate, and while Artimus told him he didn't expect that, Artimus did seem to be hoping Jeff could offer some special insight.

Artimus directed them to a large, semi-circular couch, and the four of them sat.

"So," Artimus began, "how is the vote looking, Goldwin?"

Goldwin Bellows shook his head. "We've made some gains, up to about thirty-three solid votes supporting action, eight leaning our way and five completely undecided... but even if we get all of those thirteen votes, that only brings us to forty-six, and I can't think of any scenarios that would get us the votes we need. There are at least fifty people who are firmly on the anti-war side – so firmly I'm afraid we can't get over that hump. We'd have to have Duanan and I think that's very unlikely"

Artimus knit his brows. He had his hands clasped, and he brought his index fingers up to his mouth and bounced them against his lips.

There was a long, uncomfortable silence before Artimus spoke. "Well... I guess that's why we give these speeches. We must believe we have some hope of swaying people, don't we? I mean it's not like everyone there is so obsessed with their own speech and how they look that they don't actually listen to anything anyone else is saying."

His expression made it clear that he didn't actually believe that for a second. "Maybe we've got a real shot here."

It seemed like Artimus was trying to sell himself as much as anything. "I guess that's why we call it 'work'. I guess that's why we don't say to our families: 'I'll be back in nine hours, I'm headed to *easy*."

The others laughed uncomfortably.

Artimus turned his attention to Jeff. "Any thoughts coming to mind, Jeff?"

Jeff was at a complete loss and feeling very uncomfortable. *What does he expect from me?* "Uh... no." He shook his head. "I'm afraid I don't have any suggestions." He felt like he was letting Artimus down in some way, but he had no idea what Artimus even wanted.

Artimus put his hand on Jeff's shoulder and smiled. "Okay. Just try to keep your mind open, and if anything comes to you, please let me know."

Chapter 25:

The council chamber was a grand room.

Jeff squinted at the intricate details on the vaulted ceiling and nearly stumbled. Artimus caught him by the elbow and steadied him.

"Sorry," Jeff mumbled.

Artimus led him down to the very front row and gestured for him to sit. Each council person had a box with two seats. Each box was separated by several feet.

Jeff looked around the chamber at the others sitting properly in their individual boxes.

"There are one-hundred council people," Artimus explained, "each with one vote. Governor Duanan heads the council and has twenty-one votes." Artimus pointed to a man seated at the center of a long table at the front of the chamber. There were chairs behind the table arranged so they faced the rest of the chamber. The table was on a platform above and behind a lectern that was also oriented so that the speaker faced the rest of the chamber. "He's a good guy, but he and I are on opposite sides of this issue.

"There are thirty speeches scheduled today. I'll be speaking twenty-ninth, and Duanan will be speaking thirtieth. Now, unfortunately, as a member of the Armed Conflict Committee, I'm going to have to sit at the table up there with Duanan, so you'll be stuck here by yourself. There are bathrooms, drinks and light snacks out in the lobby. If you need to take a break, try to go in between speakers."

Jeff nodded.

"Wish me luck."

"Good luck," Jeff said.

By the fifth speech, Jeff was getting restless. Like those in Washington, the speakers seemed to have particular gifts for using a lot of words while saying very little.

"The preponderance of information, while being substantial and weighty – by nearly any reasonable measure we might apply – must also be considered with an eye toward the things we don't know... or might know but don't recognize exactly what it is we know... or understand... or perceive as that which truly matters in times such as these..."

Jeff's brain was clawing madly at his skull for some sort of escape.

Thankfully the speeches were brief. Jeff guessed that there was some sort of time limit because the speakers didn't seem like the types to relinquish the lectern easily.

As the speaker seemed to be wrapping up, Jeff shifted his weight toward the front of his seat. He planned to take the opportunity to make an escape and get something to eat.

"So in closing, let me once more state just how important it is for ALL information to be considered with the utmost care and purposefulness... for without perspective, we can't begin to establish a point at which we can *truly* understand exactly where this information leads us or places us at this point in time relative to everything else that is, or isn't, known regarding the things we believe, or hope to believe, based on things we may not fully understand, or acknowledge, in a context of a greater scheme... or environment... that doesn't completely justify the beliefs that we hope to engender, or amplify within ourselves, or within the hearts and minds of others..."

Jeff's brain began taking a pick-axe to his skull. *He... said... he... was... closing.*

After several more minutes of incomprehensible blather, the speaker gathered his notes and stepped away from the lectern.

Jeff took the opportunity to quickly but quietly make his way toward the lobby. He had the uncomfortable feeling that curious eyes were scanning him as he walked the upward-sloping walkway between boxes.

He felt a brief moment of relief as he passed through the doors into the freedom of the lobby but soon realized there were just as many curious onlookers there.

Jeff avoided eye contact as he picked up a small plate and loaded it with assorted hors d'oeuvres.

He made his way through the people who were milling about and headed toward a corner that seemed relatively empty. While he kept his eyes down, he could still sense people looking, gesturing subtly toward him and whispering.

He soon found himself longing for the boring but safely secluded environment of the council chamber.

After a few minutes of peace, he saw two council members making their way toward him. Jeff focused on his food, but they wouldn't be deterred.

"Hello, I'm Councilman Hendricks, and this is Councilman Jackson," the taller one said as he extended a hand.

Jeff quickly and awkwardly wiped his hand on his pants, and then shook each of the councilmen's hands. He tried to hide his cringe when he received a limp, dead-fish handshake from Hendricks.

"Jeff Browning."

"Good to meet you Jeff," Hendricks said. "Are you here with someone? I guess that's a silly question unless they lowered the minimum age and no-one told me."

Hendricks laughed lightly at his 'joke', and Jackson joined in politely. Jeff considered faking a laugh but realized, by the time he had thought it through, it was too late to seem natural.

Jeff was having trouble taking his eyes off several strands of hair that seemed to be glued to Jackson's forehead in a strange pattern. "I'm here with Artimus Winfred," he said.

"Ahhhh, Winfred," Jackson said, "good man, good man."

He smiled broadly, and Jeff noticed a green, leafy vegetable in his teeth.

"Very brave man, Artimus," Jackson continued. "I'm afraid he's going to have trouble with this vote though." He frowned and shook his head. "Too bad, too bad."

The voice in the back of Jeff's head was telling him Jackson was full of it. He wanted the vote to go against Artimus, and Jeff even sensed that Jackson would get some personal satisfaction in seeing Artimus lose. It went beyond just wanting the vote to go one way or the other.

Jackson didn't like Artimus.

He was smiling again, and the green spot on his tooth was driving Jeff crazy.

"Excuse me. I should be getting back." Jeff moved toward the chamber door.

Both Hendricks and Jackson made subtle sour expressions, and Jeff could tell they weren't happy about being brushed off. He could tell – and he wasn't sure how much of this was the strange 'sense' he was experiencing and how much was simple body language – that both of them considered themselves too important to be taken so lightly by a *boy* like Jeff.

Jeff didn't give a damn.

He pushed past them, dropped his plate in a pile of dirty dishes and made his way to a small line that had formed outside the chamber doors waiting for the current speech to end.

When the doors opened, Jeff made his way back to Artimus' box and dozed through the remaining speeches.

When Artimus finally stepped up, Jeff perked up. He was very curious about what Artimus would say.

Artimus stepped up to the microphone, and with little fanfare, began.

"Esteemed councilmen and councilwomen, twenty-five years ago I fought to free us from the tyranny of Doclotnurian rule. I watched friends and family die at their hands. And many of theirs died at these hands." He paused and looked down at his hands as he held them out away from his body with palms facing upward.

"Those wounds are deep, and they take a long time to heal. And when they heal, the flesh may never be the same again."

He paused for several moments, and when he spoke again, he did so with a force and conviction that shook Jeff.

"BUT THESE WOUNDS MUST HEAL."

Again he paused, and when next he spoke, his voice had taken on a much softer and more conciliatory tone.

"Our brothers... our forebears... need... our help. They face desperate times."

Pause.

"When you strip away the conflict... the petty differences... they... are... US." Artimus pointed at himself with his hands.

"Who among us has not had moments of anger... moments of *fury* with family members? Yet we will always be family. That doesn't end just because we've had hard times.

"And when someone... an outsider tries to hurt that loved one, we band together... even if the last words we've spoken to that loved one were in anger.

"Ladies and Gentleman, if this cause isn't worth fighting for, I don't believe we will ever find a cause worth fighting for.

"Thank you for your time."

Artimus' speech was the shortest of the day. Jeff assumed that this whole session was something of a 'summary' and much more had been discussed and debated in previous sessions.

Artimus went back to his seat, and Governor Duanan got up to give the final speech. Jeff got his first good look at Duanan. He was a large, pudgy man with white hair. He didn't look well – not overtly sick, but not well either. He looked like the sort of person who, if he had to climb a flight of steps, would end up red faced, sweaty and needing rest.

Jeff got the sort of feeling that he was noticing in certain situations. A sense for the nature of the person, and the one he had at that mment wasn't good. He had a strong feeling that Duanan was a person he shouldn't trust.

Artimus said he was a good man, so Jeff decided to try to keep an open mind.

After all, he was a politician, so even if he tortured puppies in his spare time, that might not make him a bad guy... compared to other politicians.

Duanan stepped to the lectern and paused. He seemed to be holding back a smile – as if he took some pleasure in being the center of attention but didn't want to be too obvious about it.

"When I was a young boy, growing up on one of the... smaller farms of the west end pastures," he began, "my father and I used to sit on the porch as the sun was going down, and he'd say to me: 'Son, one day I hope you'll grow up to be strong and wise... and I hope you'll know the right thing to do even when there are no easy answers.'

"Well." The smile came again, but this time he did a poorer job of hiding it. "I think my father would be proud of what his little boy has been able to achieve." He looked up at the vaulted ceiling and paused for a moment.

"And if my father could be with us now – wise man that he was – one thing I can be sure of is that he would not want us sacrificing the lives of our children... our *children*... for the Doclotnurians." He made a sour expression when he said the word 'Doclotnurians' as if the word itself left a bad taste in his mouth.

"The Doclotnurians may look like us, they may talk like us, they may share some ancient history with us...

"But they're not us.

"What do we owe those... *people*?" The emphasis in his last word seemed to question if they were even people.

"What do we owe a civilization that had no respect for us or our freedom? What do we owe people who killed, maimed, and tortured our bravest just to try to maintain their unjust hold over us?

"What do we owe them? We... owe... them... NOTHING.

"I have not forgotten the atrocities committed by the Doclotnurians. Some will say that was a long time ago. It doesn't seem all that long ago to me. Some may say it's wrong to not forgive after this time. I say it would be a dishonor to the sacrifices of our brave men and women to forgive too easily.

"Some of those who have spoken today are very brave... brave with the lives of our children. None of them will be carrying a gun, you can bet that." He smirked and paused for effect.

"I'm a strong man, I'm a determined man." His eyes drifted down, and he paused. "I'm a... peaceful man. I will use all of my strength and my determination to maintain peace."

He collected his notes and returned to his seat. Jeff had to admit to himself, as much as his senses told him to dismiss this man and, as much as he looked like someone who was full of himself, he did make some good points. Jeff was sure that his father would always argue for peace.

Always? Jeff wondered what his father would have said in 1941.

A man in a black suit with a deep, booming voice stepped to the lectern. The man had made some previous procedural announcements, and Jeff assumed he was some sort of coordinator / organizer. Jeff wasn't sure if he was an actual councilman, but there was something in his manner – a clear, humble professionalism – that made him guess he wasn't. "Voting will occur promptly at six o'clock."

After that announcement there was a bustle of activity as the council members rose and milled about.

Some left the chamber, some conversed with colleagues, and others busied themselves shuffling papers." Artimus came from his table and sat with Jeff.

"Any thoughts, comments?" he asked Jeff.

Jeff wasn't sure what he wanted from him. Did he just want reassurance? Jeff felt like he was just there to be there but otherwise completely useless – like man-nipples. "Your speech went great." Jeff tried to add some enthusiasm to his voice, but he wasn't sure that he was successful.

Artimus smiled. "Thanks." He looked around the room. "I'm afraid it wasn't enough though."

Alvina Royer and Goldwin Bellows joined them.

"Great job," Alvina said.

"Yes, very well said," Goldwin added.

"Do you think we have a chance?" Artimus asked.

Neither of them said anything. It seemed that it didn't even need to be stated.

Chapter 26:

At precisely 6:00, the man in the black suit stepped to the lectern again. "We are now voting on council bill 7654G: Authorization for Military Force in the Aid and Defense of Doclotnury." He pushed a button on the lectern, and behind him, two large signs became illuminated. One was green and labeled 'Yes', the other was red and labeled 'No'.

Jeff watched as Artimus pressed a green 'Yes' button at his desk. The green and red signs on the far wall were both quickly counting up. After a minute or two, it seemed that the counting had stopped.

Artimus clearly wasn't happy. There were 42 'Yes' votes and 55 'No' votes.

"We'll have to wait a few minutes until everyone who's voting has had their choice, and then Duanan will announce his vote." Artimus explained.

"What are the chances he'll vote your way?" Jeff asked.

Artimus smiled. "About the same as him stripping naked, asking one of the ushers to swat his bare bottom and singing 'I'm a Little Dandy'... still we can hope."

Jeff thought a moment. "Hope he'll vote your way or hope he'll strip naked and ask one of the ushers to swat his bare bottom?"

Artimus laughed. "Well at least the latter would be some consolation for the vote not going our way."

After several minutes, an annoying electric tone signaled the closing of the Vote.

Jeff waited for Duanan to cast his vote... and waited... and waited. The room was silent and tense, but Duanan kept them waiting.

It must make him feel very important, Jeff thought. Jeff was beginning to wonder what Artimus liked about him.

He seemed like a jerk from what Jeff could see.

Finally, Duanan rose and walked slowly to the lectern.

He stood at the lectern and continued the theater. He lowered his head solemnly and pretended to be in deep deliberation. Jeff assumed he was really thinking about the groceries he needed to pick up on the way home.

"And I," he finally spoke, "vote in favor of peace... I vote NO." He lowered his head and walked slowly away as if he had just made the most difficult, solemn decision of his life, but Jeff thought he could sense the absolute JOY that Duanan felt at that moment.

The man in the black suit stepped to the lectern one last time. "Session dismissed," he said in a booming voice, and the assembled crowd started to file out.

Jeff began to get up, but Artimus put his hand on his arm. "It will be a lot easier if we just give it a minute to clear out," Artimus said. Then he turned away and shook his head. "Damn," he said under his breath.

Soon the chamber was nearly empty, and Jeff and Artimus made their way out. Artimus was uncomfortably quiet. Jeff felt tempted to try to make small talk just to break the silence, but he wasn't sure if it was appropriate.

They walked in near silence back to Artimus' office.

Artimus sat heavily behind his desk. Jeff took a seat in a chair off to the side. Artimus sat for a few moments just staring, and Jeff was getting more and more uncomfortable. He hadn't seen Artimus like this. Since he had first met him, it seemed that Artimus was always smiling, joking, laughing – at that moment he looked as if his dog had just died.

"I'm sorry," Artimus said after several minutes. "Let me just check my messages, and we can head home."

He tapped on a screen that was built into his desk, and the light flickered on his face. His fingers tapped around the screen in what seemed like a random pattern, but Jeff assumed he was typing out some quick responses.

After about ten minutes, he turned off the screen,

pulled a protective panel over it and got up. "Okay, ready to go?"

"Sure," Jeff said.

"I'm headed home, Codi," Artimus said.

"Good night," Codi's voice said over hidden speakers.

Artimus led Jeff back into the garage, and the car doors opened right on cue.

"Sometimes I just wonder if it's all worth it," Artimus said as he got in behind the controls. "I'm sorry. I shouldn't be bothering you with this... it's just frustrating. Maybe I should relax, and let them all go to hell."

Chapter 27:

Once Artimus was in the kitchen, he quickly returned to his old self. As Jeff sat at the table and tried to stay out of the way, Baldwin, Nahima and Artimus were having a towel fight. Baldwin and Nahima had teamed up against Artimus and were coming at him from both sides, but Artimus was holding his own.

"Okay, I have a philosophical question," Nahima said as she snapped her towel at Artimus who deftly side-stepped it.

"What's that?" Artimus asked. "Owww..."

Baldwin got a good shot in at the back of Artimus' neck as he was distracted. Artimus turned his attention to Baldwin but kept one eye on Nahima.

"You and Mom knew each other since elementary school, right?" she asked.

"Yes..." Artimus got a quick shot in at Nahima and then turned his attention back to Baldwin.

"So if you looked at an old photograph when she was a little girl, and thought that she was attractive, would that be romantic... or really creepy?"

There was a strange beeping sound. At first Jeff thought it was some sort of timer for their dinner, but then realized it was a telephone – or something very similar – ringing. Artimus dropped his towel on a chair and headed over to a wall panel shaking his head.

"I don't know where you think of these things." Artimus pushed a button on the panel. "Yes?"

Jeff could see a small video image of the councilman he had met earlier, Goldwin, on a screen in the center of the panel.

"Turn on the video events channel," Goldwin said.

"What's going on?" Artimus asked. "Something about today's vote?"

"I'm not sure if I can explain," Goldwin said. "Why don't you check it out for yourself, and then I'll talk to you later."

"Sure," Artimus said. "I'll talk to you later." He pushed a button and the image disappeared.

The four of them walked to the other room.

"Video on," Artimus said in a clear precise voice, "link thirty-seven."

A small projector popped down from a hidden panel in the ceiling and began projecting an image of a news show on a blank wall.

An attractive woman was talking to an older gentleman. "Is there any chance these images have been faked in some way?" she asked him.

"That's certainly a possibility that we have to keep in mind. We generally haven't thought that they would have the technology to fake these images, but of course, we wouldn't have thought they had the technology that they seem to show in the video either. One way or another, they have technology of which we were previously unaware," he answered.

"Let's show our viewers that video one more time."

Jeff's stomach clenched into a tight knot. He was looking at the creature from his dreams, a pheerion.

The pheerion was speaking... in the same wheezing, croaking voice Jeff had heard in his dream the night before. As he spoke, subtitles crawled across the screen translating: "We have strengths that you do not yet know."

Jeff realized that, as in his dream last night, there was something in his mind that seemed to be translating the words for him. He felt that he could understand the words even without the sub-titles, but he was sure it wasn't an actual audible translation. It was in his mind. He closed his eyes just to see if he could still understand without reading the words.

"We ask for immediate unconditional surrender. If

our demands are not met..."

Yes! Yes, he could understand even without the subtitles. He opened his eyes and was looking at a grainy image of a forest.

"We will now demonstrate the power of our ultimate weapon."

The camera panned back, and Jeff could see a large gun. The barrel of the gun was about ten feet long, and twelve inches in diameter. While it didn't look like a traditional gun – it had hoses and tubes and other electronic devices attached to it – the general size and shape made it clear to be a cannon of some sort.

The pheerion stepped behind the gun, grasped two handles and plugged some sort of key into it. The gun hummed to life. The pheerion swiveled it toward the forest, pushed a button and...

A spectacular wave of energy erupted from the gun. The energy beam caused a blurring and distortion of everything that they had previously seen clearly beyond it. It was like looking through water that had waves moving across the surface.

The distortion stopped and was replaced by a cloud of debris. As that debris slowly settled and cleared, Jeff's mouth fell open.

The forest - acres and acres of trees - had been completely... *flattened.*

Jeff looked at the others to see if they were as shocked as he was, and if anything, they seemed more shocked.

Artimus was just staring at the screen. He was intently focused on it, seemingly oblivious of everything else. Nahima and Baldwin had similar expressions.

The pheerion spoke again, but this time he wasn't on screen. He likely didn't want his image to distract from the devastation. "We would prefer to settle all this peacefully, but if we have no choice, we will use this weapon."

The video ended and the woman and man came back

on screen.

"Volume two," Artimus said and the volume dropped. "Well that's... dramatic," he said.

He seemed to be thinking. Nahima and Baldwin weren't saying anything. They were looking at each other, then at Artimus, then at the screen.

"Let's have some dinner," Artimus said, breaking the silence. "I have a feeling tomorrow is going to be a busy day."

Chapter 28:

Dinner was uncomfortably quiet.

"After dinner," Artimus said without raising his eyes from the food he was working on, "I'd like to show you something, Jeff."

Nahima and Baldwin looked at each other. Jeff had the definite, uncomfortable feeling that everyone else knew something that he didn't. Actually, he knew there were *many* things that they knew that he didn't, but in this case, he felt that it had something to do with him.

They went back to eating in silence, and the silence began to gnaw at Jeff. *What's going on? What is Artimus going to show me? Damn it! Why am I the only one who doesn't seem to have a clue what's going on?*

After several minutes, it was really getting to him. "What are you going to show me?" he finally asked.

Artimus stopped eating and made eye contact with Jeff. "It's... complicated. Let's just relax and enjoy our meal." He smiled.

A smile that seemed too forced to Jeff, but he didn't know if he had any real choice but to keep eating. He couldn't *demand* that Artimus tell him, could he?

He still felt a little guilty for lying to them about himself as long as he did. It seemed he was getting a taste of his own medicine.

He tried to finish his food, but his stomach was twisting. He found it hard to eat. *Did it have something to do with that news report? It certainly seemed to shake everybody up. But why did Artimus have something specifically to show Jeff and why did the others seem to know what was coming?*

Jeff found himself looking around the table, and the marked lack of eyes that were willing to meet his just put him more on edge.

Eventually, everyone finished. They all looked

around at each other waiting for the next step.

Artimus finally broke the silence. "Would you two mind cleaning up?" he asked Baldwin and Nahima. "I'd like to fill Jeff in on some of those other details."

Nahima and Baldwin nodded and began collecting plates.

"Jeff. Come with me. I think you'll find this interesting."

Chapter 29:

Artimus led him to a room Jeff had not previously seen. The first thing Jeff noticed was that this particular room was *filled* with the decorative ovals that Jeff had seen all over the house.

Artimus led him to a desk, grabbed a thin panel in the desk and slid it out. There were 14 bulleted sentences / paragraphs.

"These," Artimus said importantly, "are the 14 prophecies."

He ran his hand down the sentences and then stepped back to give Jeff some time to read them:

1. When times seem most dire, the Raja will fall from the sky.

2. The Raja will have strength and vision that even he won't recognize.

3. The Shaman will die for the one he loves, but his actions will come far too late to save the one he loves from the same fate.

4. At the end of the great, human/pheerion war, pheerion and human will be ready to share the planet and live together in peace and harmony.

5. While The Raja will wield great power, he will require the guidance of the Shaman to reach his destiny.

6. Few will recognize The Raja for who he is.

7. As the most fearsome battle rages, The Raja

must go to the heart of darkness. The heart must be killed to stop the beast.

8. The Raja will bear the Numino.

9. When humans fight humans, they risk all, but the battle can't be avoided. Some will sacrifice all, and their sacrifices must not be in vain. The Raja must remember this and not be too distracted to help those whose hearts are true defeat those who betray their own.

10. The Raja's compassion and trust will earn him allies. Those allies will be keys to victory.

11. Only The Raja has the power to wrest the Numino from the Warlord.

12. The enigma will baffle all but The Raja. To him, it will be a child's game.

13. Only after they have fulfilled their destiny will the Child and Raja depart.

14. The Child and the land are one. As long as the Child suffers, so will the land.

Artimus watched Jeff's face as he read and waited expectantly as he was finishing.

Jeff wasn't sure what to say. It all seemed like a lot of crap to him, but he didn't want to insult Artimus' faith. It seemed that he took the nonsense very seriously.

So that's it? He thinks I'm the 'Raja' because I 'fell from the sky'? These prophecies are just broad, vague generalizations, like fortune cookies, horoscopes... or a Nostradamus 'prediction'.

Artimus seemed to be trying to calculate the best way of explaining it all. "If you can bear with me, I'll try to

117

explain... starting from the beginning."

He scratched the back of his neck. Artimus' discomfort was making Jeff uncomfortable.

"Our... recorded... history starts a little over 500 years ago. We were... uncivilized... at that point. It's not clear if we had any methods of communication. That has been a point of debate among historians. It's also not clear where we came from. That's also been widely debated, though more theologically than historically.

"There was a... man... The Elder... who taught us. He taught us our language. He taught us to read and write. He taught us about mathematics and materials, manufacturing etcetera. We learned and advanced and developed and became a much more advanced society, and as we advanced, The Elder became less active in his guidance.

"The nature of The Elder is another topic that is debated. The Elder, himself, claimed to simply be a knowledgeable man with some special abilities, though some people want to elevate him to the level of a god. We, in the church, believe that idea to be sacrilegious. The elder taught us that it was for us to find the nature of God ourselves. But we, in the church, do feel the elder is a very important figure, just not directly associated with God. Some of us think he may have been a visitor from another world."

Artimus looked at Jeff, before continuing.

"It's unclear how much of what we know about the Elder is myth and how much is fact. According to some sources, he lived for more than 200 years without any physical signs of aging. Some claim that the records are incomplete and exaggerated. In fact, there are no photographs, recordings, video or any other firm evidence that The Elder existed, just stories that have passed from generation to generation.

"Most agree that he existed, but many think he was simply a man – though certainly a very wise man – who added to our knowledge but didn't have any special powers. There are no records of The Elder beyond about the year 200."

Artimus stopped to try to see how all that was being received. "Are you following me so far?"

Jeff nodded. "Very interesting." He was getting increasingly uncomfortable. He felt Artimus was assuming far too much and contorting Jeff to fit some mythology of their culture. It explained Artimus' behavior since Jeff had told them who he was, but the whole situation put Jeff in an awkward situation.

I know I'm not this 'Raja', but Artimus seems convinced I am. How can I get him to see the truth? Will it crush him after he has gotten his hopes up? I can't continue to let him think this. I don't have any special abilities or insight...

Artimus gestured to the ovals all around the room. "Do you recognize these?"

"Sure," Jeff shrugged. "I noticed they seem to be common in your art-work."

"We call them 'Numinos'." Artimus explained. "Do they remind you of anything?"

Jeff shrugged again. "Decorated eggs... I don't know."

"May I... see your locket?" Artimus pointed at the chain around Jeff's neck.

Jeff pulled it out and handed it to him.

Artimus paused and looked intently at it. He seemed to be acting very strangely. He seemed afraid he might break it. He slowly lifted it and held it in front of a two-foot tall wooden oval that was hanging on the wall

Then Jeff saw it.

The shapes and designs of the ovals that were all around the house looked similar to the design that was engraved in his locket. He hadn't noticed it before, but now that he saw it, the similarities were a little eerie.

Artimus gave the locket back to Jeff, and the two of them stood silently for a few minutes. It was as if Artimus had something else he wanted to say, but he was having trouble finding the words.

He put his hands on the large wooden oval which had a split down the middle. Artimus paused he seemed unsure what do next. After a few awkward moments he swung the two halves – which were like doors on a cabinet – open.

Jeff stared.

Inside the 'cabinet' was a sketch that looked similar to the photo of Jeff's father that was in his locket – similar but not exact. It was almost like a police sketch.

Jeff was confused. "Why did you draw that?" he asked.

Artimus looked at him and seemed to also be confused for a moment. "I didn't draw it. The Prophet drew it."

"The Prophet?" Jeff looked at him as if he had just announced that he was 'Zarthur, queen of the newts'.

Why'd he have someone draw the photo? And if he wanted a sketch, I could have lent the locket to him so he could have drawn it more exact.

"The Prophet drew this," Artimus said as he pointed at the sketch, "approximately sixty-five years ago. According to the prophet, this is an image of The Elder."

Jeff started to get it.

He pointed at the sketch, and words failed him for a minute. "Are are you saying this was drawn *before* you saw the locket?!"

Artimus nodded. "Long before I saw it. That's right."

Jeff opened the locket, examined the photo and then squinted at the sketch. It was close, but not exact.

Could the resemblance just be coincidence?

Jeff remembered seeing an amusing photo in which a newscaster looked very similar to the police artist sketch that was being shown behind him.

And what about the other patterns that seemed similar to the locket? That is an odd combination of coincidences.

But unusual things do happen.

The locket probably isn't even sixty-five years old, and my father certainly isn't...

"What's this all mean?" Jeff asked. He turned and looked at Artimus. He tried to read his face.

Artimus looked back at him. Again, he seemed to be measuring his words. "I ... and I need to say, there are obviously far more things that I don't know than I do know... but I think your father may be The Elder, and you may be the Raja."

Jeff shook his head and looked back at the sketch. "That's impossible. My father only disappeared a little over a year ago. . . How long are your 'years' here, anyway?"

"375 days" Artimus answered.

"So there's no way my father could have been here 500 years ago or even sixty-five years ago."

Artimus put his hand on his shoulder. "I can't even pretend to have all the answers. There are things you and I can't fully understand and may never fully understand, but I think you're very special. Maybe your father isn't The Elder, but the prophet drew this image." He pointed at the sketch. "Maybe you, and maybe your father are important for reasons we don't understand. Maybe..." He stopped at that point and seemed to be thinking.

"What?" Jeff asked.

"Well, are you sure what you remember of your home world is real?"

That seemed a strange question to ask. If it was possible any world wasn't real, Jeff felt it was the one he was in. "How could my world not be real?" Artimus shook his head. "I don't know. I'm afraid I don't have the answers I'd like to have. I was just wondering if maybe you were born from the stars, and those memories you have are just something ... I don't know."

At that point, Jeff couldn't resist laughing. "You

know, all this is starting to sound a little..."

"Silly?" Artimus flushed. "Yeah, I guess it all could seem a little silly. I'm sorry. I wish I could offer more. I just think... I think there's something very important about you. Nahima thinks so, and she has always had a very good sense for these things."

The two of them stood in silence for several minutes.

Jeff had somewhat mixed feelings. He thought all of it sounded very strange. Most likely just some odd coincidence... *still... could this have something to do with my father? My father may not be The Elder, but maybe The Prophet was somehow able to predict that he would arrive at some point. Is it at least a clue that I may be able to find him?*

Jeff was sure he wasn't as important as Artimus thought he was, but there was at least something unusual going on.

Considering how improbable the past few days had been, *is it really so amazing that a drawing from some 'prophet' would look similar – not identical, but similar – to my father?*

"Well. I don't know if it's important that you believe it. As long as you can keep an open mind, let's see what happens. No matter what, I'm glad you're here." Artimus grabbed Jeff and hugged him, and Jeff endured it somewhat awkwardly.

Chapter 30:

"We have a saying," Artimus said as he led Jeff, Baldwin and Nahima down into a basement, "always come to the peace table well-armed."

Artimus flipped a few switches, and bright lights illuminated what Jeff inferred to be a shooting range.

"I'm not a big fan of guns." As Artimus spoke, he flipped another switch, and a panel lifted revealing an enormous assortment of all shapes and sizes of guns.

Jeff almost laughed out loud at the irony of Artimus' claim combined with the collection he had just revealed. It would be like walking into someone's wine cellar, observing thousands of bottles of wine and hearing them say: 'I don't drink' or being led to a basement full of dead bodies and hearing: 'I don't really enjoy killing and hearing gasping screams for help accompanied by the sounds of tendons ripping and bones snapping.'

"But around here, guns are something of a necessary evil," Artimus finished his thought.

He selected a large hand-gun – roughly the size of a .357 magnum with a ten-inch barrel, though it was much more futuristic looking. Artimus examined one side then the other before leading the others to an area that seemed designed to be a firing position about thirty feet from a row of targets.

"Do you have guns where you're from?" Artimus asked.

Jeff nodded. His grandfather was something of a collector, and Jeff had a good bit of experience handling and firing guns. Though the ones Artimus had shown him were very different from anything with which he was familiar.

Artimus held the pistol grip with his right hand and flipped a small sliding switch between its two positions with his thumb. "This is the safety. Off... on... off... on." He watched Jeff's face to make sure he was following. "The weapon won't discharge when the safety's on, and the safety will be on at all times unless you have immediate plans to discharge. Are you right-handed?"

Jeff nodded.

Artimus pushed a button with his thumb, and a battery dropped out of the hand grip into his left hand. He handed the gun to Jeff and seemed pleased with the way Jeff handled it. "Good, GOOD, always keep it pointed away from anyone you don't intend to shoot. You have some experience, don't you?"

Jeff nodded. "Not with anything like this though."

"Switch the safety off and on a few times. Get the feel for it."

Jeff complied and looked over some of the other details as he switched the safety between positions.

Artimus showed him the battery. "This is the power-supply." He handed it to Jeff. "Is the safety off or on?"

"On." Jeff answered.

Artimus nodded. "Good. Now did you see how I took the battery out?"

Jeff nodded.

"It slides up and snaps into place, then you can release it, and drop it out to replace it with a fresh one using this thumb switch." Artimus pointed to the button he had pushed to drop the battery. "Put it in and take it out a few times."

Jeff snapped the battery in, then pushed the button and dropped it into his hand. He snapped it back up and then dropped it again, getting a little more comfortable each time.

"Good, very good. Okay, put the battery in and leave it."

Jeff snapped the battery into place.

"This," Artimus said as he pointed to a small needle in the area where the hammer of a more traditional gun would have been, "is your power level. All the way right is 'full', all the way left is 'empty'."

Jeff noted that it was approximately 80% full.

"You can illuminate the charge indicator," Artimus clicked a switch near the needle, and a dim light came on. "But it's not a good idea to keep the light on. In the dark, you can be spotted by any light you might be giving off. This dial here," Artimus pointed to a round dial that had settings numbered 1-10. "Is the power setting." He clicked it through a number of settings. "Setting 1," Artimus clicked the dial to '1', "is the lowest setting and enough to stun and disorient most people. If you hit a small child with a '1' setting, you'll likely kill him or her."

Jeff was a little uncomfortable with that bit of bluntness, and he looked at Artimus who seemed different than Jeff had seen him before. Jeff suspected he was seeing 'soldier Artimus' for the first time.

Artimus met Jeff's eyes. He seemed to know that Jeff was a little uncomfortable but plowed ahead. "Setting 3." He clicked it into position '3'. "Will kill most humans, but if you're shooting at humans and intending on killing them, use 5," he clicked the dial two more positions, "to make sure."

Again their eyes met, and again Artimus looked back at Jeff with a detached stoicism.

"Setting 3 will stun a pheerion, and setting 8 should be enough to kill one, but use 10..." Artimus clicked it to the maximum setting.

"To make sure," Jeff finished his thought for him.

"Right." Artimus allowed himself a brief smile.

Jeff wasn't sure which made him more uncomfortable – the thought of shooting to kill humans, or the thought that he might actually have to face down a pheerion.

"Each full battery will give you approximately fifty shots at power '10' or five-hundred shots at power '1'. Those are the basics. Do you think you have all that?" Artimus asked.

Jeff nodded.

Artimus looked him in the eye and seemed satisfied that he really did have it. "Good. Let's do some shooting. Baldwin? Start us out."

He handed Baldwin the gun, and Baldwin clicked the power knob down to '1'.

"Now," Artimus addressed Jeff, "watch what Baldwin does. He's going to have a firm grip, he wants to control the gun, but he wants to be careful to not grip too firmly." Artimus clenched his fists tightly around an imaginary gun. "If you clench too tightly, your tense muscles can cause vibration. He's going to take a deep breath, let some of that out, and then pause timed to when he's ready to shoot. At the point when he pulls the trigger, he won't be breathing either in or out. Everything should be as relaxed as possible. You want to try not to flinch as you shoot, and continue aiming even after you've pulled the trigger for a few moments. People sometimes anticipate the shot and pull the gun back before the shot has actually left the gun. Okay Baldwin, go ahead."

Baldwin aimed at the first target on the left. The gun flashed and the target - thirty feet away – flashed seemingly simultaneous with the shot. A '7' lit above the target.

"Good," Artimus said. "The target has ten zones. Ten is the center and one is the outer ring. At this distance, a '7' is very good."

Baldwin grinned. Then he lined up and shot at the second target: Another '7', then a '6', then an '8'.

"Very nice," Artimus looked impressed. "That's a... twenty-eight."

Baldwin clicked the safety into the 'on' position and handed the gun – butt first – to Artimus who had extended his hand.

Artimus stepped into position and pushed a button on the table that cleared all Baldwin's scores before raising the gun. He registered an '8', then '9', then '8', then '7'. He clicked the safety and did some quick addition. "Let's see... that's thirty-two."

Nahima stepped up and took the gun from Artimus. She winked at Jeff and said: "Now if the boys are done playing, I'll show you how this is really done."

For a brief moment, Nahima appeared to Jeff to be one of the sexiest women he had ever seen, and – while a 14 year old boy might find an overweight, toothless middle-aged woman sexy under the right conditions – Nahima's appeal went beyond pure adolescent hormones.

But Jeff had other things on his mind, and the feeling quickly passed.

Nahima took a stance, and taking much less time than either Baldwin or Artimus, she squeezed off a '9' then '10', then '9' and '9'.

Artimus nodded approvingly. "Thirty-seven, excellent as always. You feel ready, Jeff?"

Jeff nodded and stepped tentatively forward. He took the gun from Nahima, clicked the safety 'off' and raised the gun. It felt odd in his hand. Compared to similarly sized guns he had handled before, it was much lighter. He gripped it tightly, and then, remembering Artimus' instruction, he tried to relax.

He focused on his breathing as he sighted in the target. *Out, in, out, in... let some out and hold.*

He pulled the trigger, and from behind the gun, he could see the shot all the way from the gun to the target, and then he saw a '9' light above the target. He fought to hold back a grin. He didn't want to look cocky, and he realized it was likely beginner's luck.

He repeated the procedure with the next target, and this time got a '10', then a '9', then another '10'. After that, he couldn't hold back the grin anymore, and it split his face, straining the muscles that were trying to hold it back.

Nahima and Baldwin were staring open-mouthed, and Artimus had a grin nearly as big as Jeff's. He put a hand on Jeff's shoulder and said: "Well if you're not The

Raja, you're at least a good enough shot to help us out."

Chapter 31:

As Jeff prepared for bed, he realized that he had never had so many conflicting emotions all at once. He was hopeful and excited that his father might be alive, but he worried about his mother – alone and confused back home.

Everything he saw was fresh and new and exciting, but there seemed to be an impending war with some *creatures* that were more frightening than anything Jeff had to deal with in 21st century Earth.

This family who had taken him in was kind and gracious, but they thought he was something that he clearly wasn't.

I'm not some kind of damned savior.

He wondered what Baldwin thought about the subject. "Do you really think I'm The Raja?" he asked.

Baldwin thought for a moment and then shook his head. "No... no, I don't think so."

"Sorry," he added sheepishly.

"Don't be," Jeff said. "I'm sure I'm not The Raja."

"Here, let me show you something." Baldwin pulled his shirt part-way off exposing his shoulder.

Jeff saw a large brown spot. "What's that, some kind of scar?"

Baldwin pulled his shirt back on. "Birth mark. But did you notice what shape it is?"

Jeff shrugged. "Sort of oval."

"Like a Numino?"

"I guess." Jeff shrugged again.

"For the past ten years, I've had to put up with my father thinking I might be 'The Raja', just because it looks like I might: 'Bear the Numino'... remember Prophecy 8? The Raja will..."

"Bear the Numino," Jeff finished for him. "Yeah, I

know that one."

"I'm pretty much mediocre in everything. I'm not real smart, I'm not real strong, I'm not real brave or adventurous, I don't understand things... Nahima has way more ability than me in all those areas..."

He dropped his voice to a whisper which caused Jeff to look around wondering if there was anyone close enough to actually hear them. "Between you and me, I've sometimes wondered if she could be 'The Raja'. I know everyone assumes it's a guy, but she can do some pretty amazing things, and who knows with those prophecies. They're so vague. I've even wondered if it might be dad. Anyway, just because I have an oval birth-mark, my father thinks it might be me. Frankly, I'm just really glad you're here so he has someone else to get all weird about for a while."

Jeff felt like he was in one of those movies where each person in a line points to the next one until they get to the end, and that person is left looking for someone else to point to.

He was wishing there was someone else next to him.

Chapter 32:

Jeff looked around. He was in a... *wooden ship?* He could see the beams and planks, there was a table. It looked like an old sailing ship of some kind, but he wasn't alone.

The pheerion was there!

He looked up quickly and saw the pheerion's red, evil eyes boring into him. The pheerion spoke in his ugly, scratchy voice, and again, Jeff could understand even though the language was foreign: *'You can't stop me boy! Not while I have the power.'* The pheerion raised his hand, and Jeff stumbled back.

His eyes snapped open, and he heard Baldwin's familiar snoring.

Jeff looked at the clock: 1:90 - about the same time he had gotten up the day before.

He showered, dressed and headed to the kitchen. Again, Artimus was already dressed and at the table.

"Good morning," Artimus said. "Something to eat?"

Jeff shook his head. "I'm not really hungry this morning." He pulled out a chair and sat down. "What are we doing today?"

Artimus exhaled exaggeratedly. "I'm afraid today is going to be a tough day. We're going to have to discuss yesterday's news and see if that will change anyone's opinions of what we should do."

He leaned in and looked intently at Jeff. "I'd like to tell them about you."

Jeff was taken aback. "About... what... not that you think I'm 'The Raja'?"

Artimus nodded solemnly. "I hate to put you in that situation, but I think it's important. I think you might be the key to all this."

Jeff's stomach was in knots. Up until that point it

had been sort of odd and awkward that Artimus believed...
this ridiculous thing, but Jeff wasn't ready to be 'announced'
as The Raja. "What do you think is going to happen when
you tell people?"

Artimus shook his head. "I'm afraid I don't know.
One thing I do know is that, while many people believe...
or claim they believe... in the prophecy and the Raja, I have
a feeling very few will actually believe he's sitting in front
of them."

"I think I can imagine how they feel," Jeff said a bit
sarcastically. "Look, I don't want to hurt your feelings, but
I'm not 'The Raja'. I'd like to be able to help, but..."

Artimus smiled. "I know you don't think you are,
and maybe you're not, but please just try to keep your
mind open. That's all I can ask. Let's see what happens."

Artimus opened a small box on the table. "Here's
something else difficult that I have to ask you."

Jeff could see a tiny electronic device. There was also
some sort of white putty and a small tool.

"This," Artimus said, "is a tracking device. A small
amount of this putty can be spread on a tooth, cured, and
programmed to be read in this locator." He tapped the
electronic box. "Nahima and Baldwin both have them so
that if we ever get separated, I can track them down with
this.

"Now I understand this might sound a little... creepy
to you... and I completely understand if you don't want to
do it, and it's entirely your choice. But I have a feeling
things could get... chaotic over the coming days, and I'd
really like to make sure I can find you if something
happens."

Jeff thought that 'creepy' was an understatement.
The idea that someone would be able to track him from a
marker on his tooth was very intimidating. He looked at
Artimus.

Jeff had that re-assuring voice in the back of his head
telling him: *You can trust him*, but he still wasn't sure. *How*

do I know I can trust the voice? Jeff realized that it was probably a side effect of watching too many movies, but Artimus seemed SO trustworthy, that if Jeff was in a movie, Artimus would be the one Jeff would assume would turn out to be evil by the end of the film.

But that's silly, Jeff thought to himself. *This isn't a movie. I should trust the ones who seem trustworthy.*

He took another good look at Artimus who was waiting patiently for him to think it through. *Well if I can't trust him,* he thought, *I'm in trouble no matter what.*

"Okay. Let's do it."

Chapter 33:

The council chamber seemed much different than it had the day before. There was an anxious buzz. Artimus worked the room talking to different council-people – some that Jeff recognized and others that he didn't remember seeing before.

Jeff was seated in Artimus' box and just trying not to get in the way. Eventually Artimus made his way up to his spot behind the large table, and the proceedings began.

Many of the same people who spoke the day before spoke again. Jeff found that no-one had seemed to change their mind. Those who argued for action previously now argued that action was needed more urgently. Those who felt they shouldn't get involved still didn't see any reason to get involved – particularly now that getting involved looked more deadly.

Jeff wasn't sure exactly what Artimus had planned, and he wasn't sure if he wanted to know. After more speakers than Jeff could count, Artimus stepped up to the lectern, and Jeff's stomach started to churn.

"Respected councilmen and councilwomen," he began. "Thank you for your thoughtful words."

Artimus lowered his eyes and stood there silently for a few moments. He seemed to be finding the words – or maybe the courage – to bring up the next topic.

"I don't have a standard speech today. I think we all know times are *dire.*" *When times seem most dire, the Raja will fall from the sky.*

"Instead, I want to introduce you to someone. Jeff would you come up here please?" He extended a hand and gestured to Jeff.

There was a murmur that washed over the chamber, and Jeff began to stand. As he did so, he suddenly realized that his legs didn't have their typical strength, and he nearly collapsed back into his seat.

He made his way toward the lectern. Each step was a labor. He had to think through each step: *Right foot, left foot, right foot...*

As he arrived at the lectern, Artimus put his hand around the back of his neck and gently turned him to face the main chamber.

"This is Jeff Browning. My children found him lost in the forest a few days ago. I'd like to show you something he was carrying."

Artimus pushed a button on the lectern, and a small lamp lit. Jeff noticed another light come on behind him when that lamp illuminated. He peeked over his shoulder and saw an image of the lectern's wood grain projected on the wall behind them – over the large table of senior members.

Artimus leaned over and whispered in Jeff's ear: "May I show them the locket?"

Not like I have much choice at this point.

Jeff fished in his shirt, pulled out the locket and handed it to Artimus. Artimus opened it, put it under the lamp, and both he and Jeff turned to look over their shoulders to see the photo of Jeff's father projected on the wall behind them.

A loud gasping murmur erupted from the council chamber.

"Order, order!" Duanan commanded. "Councilman Winfred, how do you explain this outrage? Why didn't you tell me you planned these... *theatrics*?"

Artimus opened his mouth to reply, but Duanan cut him off before he could get a word out. "Take your seat." He gestured at Artimus' seat at the table beside him.

Artimus didn't move but rather stood there rigidly glaring at Duanan. Jeff noticed Duanan make a slight gesture with his hand, and armed chamber guards began to move from both sides. Artimus pulled the locket off the lectern, handed it to Jeff and said, in a quiet voice: "Just relax and tell the truth." Artimus headed for his seat. The guards stopped where they were, and the lectern began to sink into the floor.

Just behind the descending lectern, a chair rose from a place where it had been hidden below the floor. The chair faced the table at which Artimus, Duanan and the other members of the Armed Conflict committee were seated.

Duanan gestured sternly for Jeff to sit. Jeff was getting annoyed at the treatment. For a fleeting moment, he hoped that he really was 'The Raja', just so he could make a point of NOT helping people like Duanan.

Jeff sat. When he sat, a light shone in his face from a spot on the floor, and he could see an image of his face being projected on the wall behind Duanan's table. The chair was several feet below the level of the table, so Jeff had to look up to see the faces of the people who were staring intently at him.

"What did you say your name was?" Duanan asked Jeff tersely.

"I didn't."

There was scattered, nervous laughter from the chamber. Duanan's face was turning red. Jeff felt he was on the edge of erupting angrily, but he seemed to be containing himself – for the moment.

"What... is... your... name?" Duanan asked through clenched teeth.

"Jeff Browning."

"Where are your parents?"

Jeff didn't answer for a moment. He wasn't sure how to respond to that question. Artimus had advised him to be honest, so he charged ahead. "I don't know where my father is. I'm looking for him. My mother is... in another dimension. A place we call Earth."

There was a loud murmur and some laughter from the chamber. Duanan scanned the chamber sternly, and the buzzing quickly quieted.

"Ridiculous. So I take it, from your *story*, that if we run a scan, we will not find your parents as registered citizens of Caesurmia?"

"That's correct."

"Then it seems clear to me that you are likely a Doclotnurian spy with a fake Numino. You will be taken into custody, I will interview you in private, and we'll sort this out."

"YOU WILL NOT!" Artimus roared and rose from his seat. Duanan nearly tipped over in his seat, and he raised his arms to shield himself. The guards moved in – very quickly this time – and soon there were four weapons aimed directly at Artimus. Two other guards took positions on either side of Jeff. They had their hands on their guns, but they hadn't yet drawn them.

Once Duanan had some muscle to back him up, he suddenly became much more courageous. He stood up and faced Artimus. "You dare..."

Artimus was absolutely furious. Jeff had never seen him like this. It was almost as if he had inflated his body and he seemed to loom over Duanan even though he wasn't as big physically. "YOU HAVE NO RIGHT..."

"I have the right, and I have the AUTHORITY!" Duanan shot back. He was close to matching Artimus' volume, but he couldn't come close to matching the *intensity*. "You are out of order. You will stand down now, or I'll have you held for gross contempt."

Artimus looked at Jeff, then back to Duanan, then back to Jeff. Slowly, he regained his composure, and he began to deflate. His eyes still glared right through Duanan, but he backed off a bit physically.

"Take the boy to my chambers," Duanan instructed the guards.

Chapter 34:

The guards pushed Jeff roughly into Duanan's office. Jeff wasn't really resisting, but he wasn't making it easy either. If they would simply have *asked* him to come with them, he would have done so, but the more he was pushed around, the less he felt like making it easy for them.

They positioned him in front of a chair and leaned their weight on his shoulders until his knees buckled, and he slammed down into the chair. They yanked his hands behind him and shackled them behind the chair back.

The guards exited, and Jeff sat there alone for several minutes. He looked around the office. It was elaborately decorated with what Jeff assumed were very expensive, useless things. There were framed awards, and there was a large... *liquor cabinet?*... to the side of an oversized, elegant desk.

Duanan entered and closed the door loudly behind him. Jeff looked over his shoulder, and Duanan scowled at him. He walked past Jeff to the desk and tapped his finger on it several times as he made his way around to the large chair. He sat heavily and continued to stare at Jeff with an unpleasant expression.

"Who are you?" he asked in a demanding tone.

"Jeff Browning."

Duanan didn't seem happy with the answer. "Who are you *really*?"

Jeff rolled his eyes. He was trying not to get emotional and belligerent, but he was afraid he might lose that battle.

Jeff would do *anything* for anyone who asked, but he'd resist giving anything to anybody who *demanded* it.

Jeff's father was the same way. Jeff remembered two incidents that happened within a few days of each other: One rainy morning, a friend of Jeff's father called at 2:30

am and told Dr. Browning that he was stranded with car trouble and needed help. Dr. Browning was dressed and out the door within minutes after receiving the call.

A few days later, Dr. Browning's supervisor showed up at the house and wanted a project summary Jeff's father had been working on. Dr. Browning told him they were eating, and he'd have to wait. The supervisor demanded that he get the summary at that moment, and Dr. Browning calmly told him he would get it when they were done eating if the supervisor wanted to wait – an hour or two depending on how things went – or he could have it in the morning.

Jeff realized that he had inherited that trait from his father.

But Jeff wasn't sure if he could remain as cool as his father had.

"I told you my name. If you want something else, maybe you should re-phrase your question. Do you want to know what lessons I've learned that have made me who I am, or do you want to know my philosophy of life..."

"I want to know where you're from." Duanan's voice was becoming louder, and Jeff noticed that his lips continued to quiver after he had spoken.

Jeff felt like he was *sensing* Duanan. Similar to the little glimmers he had been having since he arrived indicating who he could trust and who he couldn't.

Now he seemed to be getting more detail. He was sensing Duanan's arrogance, his selfishness, his anger... *his fear?*

Yes. Jeff was getting a strong sense that Duanan was afraid of something, but he couldn't tell what.

Jeff was finding himself tempted to tell Duanan to 'go to hell', but something told him the truth would annoy Duanan more than belligerence. Jeff decided to take the route of maximum annoyance.

"I told you and the rest of the council that I'm from 'Earth'. I believe it's in an alternate dimension, but I don't know anything about what the exact relationship is... or where I am right now."

"Are you from Doclotnury?"

"No, I've never been there."

Duanan didn't seem happy with that answer. He got up from his desk and walked around behind Jeff. He grabbed Jeff's finger and began twisting it to put stress on the joint.

Intense pain shot into Jeff's finger and seemed to spread from there. Jeff grimaced but tried to avoid making too strong of a reaction.

Duanan leaned in and asked him again: "Are you from Doclotnury?"

"Noooooo... ," Jeff said as if talking to a small child. "I told you I've never been there. Did you miss that part?"

Duanan pushed harder and asked again, more loudly this time: "Are you from Doclotnury!?"

"You know," Jeff said – his voice wavering a bit from the pain. "That hurts like hell, but I'm not sure how that's going to change anything. I'm not from Doclotnury, and I've never been there."

Duanan put a little more pressure on his finger. Jeff feared something was about to snap, but then Duanan quickly released it. He walked toward his desk, fiddling with random objects distractedly.

"Are you aware," Jeff asked, "that there seems to be some kind of war brewing? Don't you have more important things to do?"

Duanan's head snapped around. "What do you know of the war?"

Jeff considered shutting up, but he knew Duanan wouldn't quit. He shook his head. "Not much."

Duanan rounded on him, and Jeff flinched. Duanan grabbed the locket that was hanging around Jeff's neck. He jerked it, and the chain snapped. Duanan examined the locket, turned it over in his hand several times and then opened it.

He looked at the photo for a good fifteen seconds. "What is this? Where did you get it? Who made it?"

"It's a locket with a photo of my father. He bought it for me and put his picture in it, but I have no idea who made it. There may be some logo or..."

Duanan slapped him hard across the face. "Don't even DARE..." His voice trailed off, and he went back to examining the locket. He looked at it from various angles and held it to the light. "Winfred must have something to do with this..." He seemed to be thinking out loud. "But he's going to be more difficult to deal with than an unregistered boy..."

He walked around and dropped the locket in a desk drawer. He pulled the chair out and sat.

There was a long pause.

Jeff tried to concentrate to see if he could get a sense for what Duanan was thinking.

He couldn't.

Jeff had been getting glimmers of insight when he hadn't been trying, but now that he *was* trying, he couldn't get anything.

Duanan tapped his fingers on the desk and seemed to be staring at a point on the wall behind and above Jeff.

After several minutes he pushed a button on his desk. "Guards, take the boy to E. L. B. prison for detention. I'll contact the warden personally to make arrangements."

Chapter 35:

Jeff spent an unpleasant hour being pushed and jostled. When he wasn't being pushed or jostled, he was sitting somewhere waiting for someone else to come along and push and jostle him some more.

They pushed and jostled him into a windowless transport where he sat on a hard metal bench. From there, they took him to the prison building where he sat on a hard wooden bench with his hands bound behind him in a large, open atrium waiting for processing.

Jeff realized that, after spending the last few days sitting on some of the most comfortable chairs he had ever experienced, he had been sitting on uncomfortable chair after uncomfortable chair ever since the hard, uncomfortable chair rose out of the floor in the council chamber.

He looked around the atrium. The building was much different than any buildings he had seen so far.

It actually was a very impressive space with vaulted ceilings. The structure itself seemed to be stone. The other structures Jeff had seen since he had arrived were made from advanced materials and had curves and textures very different from what Jeff was used to.

This building looked much more familiar to him. It had a cold, dark feeling to it – as might be expected with a prison – but Jeff still appreciated that someone had spent a lot of time and money designing and building the structure.

The area in which Jeff sat was more secure than it appeared at first glance. The room was open, but there were force-screens sealing the arched doorways to Jeff's left and right. Beyond the doorways and force-screens were more than ten guards who had nothing to do but prevent anyone who managed to get past the force-screens from going any farther. There was only one other person in there with Jeff, and his hands appeared to be bound behind his back also. Jeff inferred that he was another prisoner awaiting disposition.

Jeff fidgeted nervously wondering what to expect next. He wondered if he should have acted differently, maybe been more placating. He shook his head. *I have a feeling Duanan was out to get me from the start*, he thought. *I'd probably have ended up here no matter what.*

I probably should be pissed at Artimus. Again he shook his head. *Artimus may have gotten me into this, but that clearly wasn't what he wanted. I half expected to end up somewhere like this ever since I've been here. If anything, he just delayed the inevitable.*

Jeff fidgeted some more, tapping his feet nervously. *I wonder what's next. I guess I'll get 'booked'. Hopefully I'll get some kind of orientation or something to get an idea how this will work.*

For a moment, Jeff allowed himself a laugh at the humorous thought of an educational slideshow narrated by a whimsical cartoon otter: 'So you're in jail. Here's what you need to know...'

Jeff laughed briefly to himself before getting back to more serious thoughts... *I hope they'll put me with other juveniles or keep me alone.* He tried to not think of the more frightening possibilities.

His stomach churned violently as he wasn't quite able to completely avoid thinking about the more frightening possibilities. He felt himself beginning to flush and sweat.

He looked up at the high ceiling and tried to think about how they constructed it – anything to occupy his mind and get it off more unpleasant thoughts.

He wondered if the guy sitting ten feet down the bench could offer anything to ease his mind. He glanced over and saw that, while the man looked a little disheveled, he didn't seem like a bad guy. He looked to be in his mid-twenties. Jeff tried to see if his sense would give him any read, but again, when he really wanted it, he wasn't getting anything.

"Hey," Jeff finally said after working up the courage. "What are you in for?" It seemed like the hip, jailhouse thing to say, but as soon as it came out of his mouth, Jeff cringed and flushed with embarrassment.

The young man looked at him. "Mistaken identity," he said with an expression Jeff had trouble reading. "You?"

"I'm not sure." Jeff laughed uncomfortably.

The other man nodded as if he knew exactly what Jeff meant.

"Any idea what it's going to be like?" Jeff asked.

"First time?"

Jeff nodded.

"It's not bad – typically two to a cell. They try to match people up with people who have committed similar crimes. So unless you killed somebody," he paused and gave Jeff a good look. "You'll probably be dancy."

Jeff nodded. That was some comfort. *At least I assume 'dancy' is good. It sounds good...*

"Hey, could you do me a favor?"

Jeff paused before answering – he didn't want to have to hide a file in his rectum or anything. "What do you need?" he asked a bit nervously.

The man turned his back to Jeff. "These shackles are killing me. I think they're twisted up or something."

Jeff slid over and leaned down to look. His heart jumped momentarily as he wondered if it was some trick to get him closer so the other inmate could attack.

But then he realized he was just being paranoid. His experiences over the past several hours had made him somewhat jumpy and distrustful.

He leaned in and got a look at the shackles. They had an unusual design, but there were links of some sort that seemed to be twisted over themselves.

Jeff got a good look and then turned his back so he could get his hands on the links. With some jiggling, he could feel them loosening.

"How's that?" He asked.

The man moved his hands around some to test. "Good... great... much better. Thank you. You're a good guy."

They both turned back and tried to get themselves as comfortable as they could on the hard bench with their hands bound.

"There should be a toilet in the cell," the man said. "You'll get two meals a day through the slot in your door. Not good but edible, and once you get hungry enough, you'll find yourself looking forward to it.

"You'll be in your cell pretty much all the time, except for 20 minutes each week for a shower."

Jeff cringed. He wasn't sure why the man had originally said: 'Not bad'. If that wasn't bad, he wondered what 'bad' would be: *Maybe the same thing but with a badger gnawing on your privates.*

At least he hoped he wouldn't be in there too long. *I haven't committed any crimes... right? Artimus seems pretty important around here. He must have some pull... mustn't he? They may not believe I'm 'The Raja', but they can't have any evidence of me 'spying' on anybody.*

"Jeff Browning," a loud, precise voice snapped Jeff out of his thoughts. He rose to meet the guard who was calling him.

"John," the man on the bench said.

Jeff was confused for a moment until he realized the man was introducing himself. "Jeff," he said. "But I guess you already knew that," he added sheepishly realizing the guard had just announced his name.

John reached his hands around and Jeff realized he was trying to offer up a handshake. Jeff twisted his hands around, and the two of them shook hands awkwardly.

"Good luck," John said.

"Same to you," Jeff responded and headed toward the guard.

The guard ran Jeff through some sort of scanner (Jeff didn't have anything except his clothes – Duanan had kept the locket. His father's keys and his baseball bat – along with his original clothes - were back in Baldwin's room).

After the scan, the guard escorted him silently down a long corridor. Jeff felt like he should try to make some sort of small talk, but he had nothing to say. Two other guards joined them, and they stepped into an elevator of some sort.

No one said a word – not even the guards to one-another – and the silence was making Jeff even more nervous. The elevator doors opened, and they were in a long hallway filled with cell doors. The doors were metal with small, barred openings at eye height and slots in the bottom. The walls were stone, and the dim lighting gave the whole place a very depressing, intimidating feel.

They stopped at a door labeled "2161C". Jeff got a sudden sense of... *fear*... from guards as one inserted a key into the door and peeked through the opening.

As the door started to open, Jeff's stomach lurched at the sound of some sort of screeching guttural vocalizations. The three guards stepped with Jeff into the cell. It was darker in the cell than the hallway, but Jeff could see the rough shape of the person making the sounds. As his eyes adjusted, he could see that it was a shabby, hairy, unwashed person... with *crazy* eyes – the kind of eyes that would make Charles Manson say: "Yo, this dude is *MESSED* up."

There was also a terrible, sickening *smell*.

Jeff's 'sense' was communicating absolute, murderous RAGE. He could feel the intense emotions battering his mind. The person seemed more animal than human. Jeff tensed and stopped in his tracks.

One of the guards shoved him from behind. "Don't worry about old Oscar there. He's chained good and secure."

Jeff could see that his wrists and ankles were firmly

chained, but it was still very unsettling.

Jeff wasn't the only one who was nervous. The guards were clearly keeping their distance and staying out of the small range in which Jeff's cell-mate could move.

"If you need anything," one of the guards said, "we don't give a plooch."

The others laughed at that and then exited.

The cell door slammed loudly.

Chapter 36:

"Hey," Jeff said to his cell-mate in an attempt to make some sort of connection.

The man just glared at Jeff with wild, staring eyes and made a low, rumbling, growling sound.

"My name's Jeff, how about you?"

The man didn't acknowledge anything Jeff was saying. He just continued to make threatening, wild sounds while staring, unblinking.

Jeff tried to smile and be as un-threatening as possible, while maintaining a safe distance.

The cell was surprisingly spacious – roughly twenty-five feet by twenty-five feet. Jeff's cell-mate was restricted by his shackles to an approximately eight foot radius area in one corner, leaving plenty of room for Jeff.

There was a mat on the floor that Jeff assumed was his 'bed' and a toilet. There was also a single, dim, glowing light above the door. It gave off just enough light for someone to make their way around the cell, but it was dark – about the same level of illumination as one would have outside on a moon-lit night.

There were no exterior windows, and Jeff had the sick feeling that this illumination would be all he'd have – day and night – and there would be no way to even guess what time it was.

Jeff realized that his cell-mate... *Oscar?*... could reach the toilet. Then Jeff realized what the source of the sickening smell was.

There were little piles scattered all around Oscar's area. Many had been smashed down, but some still looked fresh.

Then the panic set in.

For a few moments Jeff felt intense, uncontrollable anxiety. He felt like he was going to throw-up or have diarrhea... or both. It was all just too much to handle. He felt as if his brain might explode from the stress. His heart pounded, he began to hyperventilate.

He concentrated on his breathing – forced himself to relax and tried to take it moment by moment. *Right now, I'm safe, I'm reasonably comfortable... I'm healthy... I can handle this... I just can't let my mind make it seem worse than it is*, he told himself.

He wondered if he should think about his father, or maybe Artimus, or maybe home and his mother. *Will that make it better... or worse?*

He sat on his mat and tried to clear his mind - tried to stay positive. *Artimus is working on getting me out of here right now*, he assured himself.

He managed to let his mind wander and soon found himself in a more relaxed state. Oscar had calmed down, but periodically he would make a grunt or growl that would snap Jeff back to reality.

He had little ability to judge time after a while. *Have I been here three hours, four hours... ten minutes?*

He heard a sound at the door, and a long paddle slid in toward Oscar.

"Put it on. Put it on!" a voice demanded. "You know you won't get any unless you do. I'm not in the mood to play games today."

Oscar put two plastic bowls on the paddle, and then the paddle retracted. A few seconds later, it re-appeared with two bowls on it. One with water and one with a gray, lumpy food of some sort.

Oscar snatched both bowls and began shoving food into his mouth. After the paddle had withdrawn again, a hand slid two more bowls under the door.

Jeff realized the other two bowls were his and moved cautiously to get them. He saw Oscar's eyes follow him the whole way, though he never stopped cramming food into his mouth.

He took the bowls back to his mat. There was a

strange sense of security on that little spot Jeff had for himself. At that moment, it was his adopted 'home'.

I guess this will be the highlight of my day. Better try to make the most of it.

There was a very long plastic spoon in the food bowl. *I guess they figure it will be difficult to make a shiv out of plastic.* The 'food' had the consistency of chopped liver and little or no smell. He took a small bite. It also had little or no taste. If anything, Jeff thought it might taste a little like rice.

He assumed it was a ground vegetable meal of some sort. After a few bites, he realized he couldn't manage much more than that. *It will probably taste better tomorrow when I'm hungrier,* he thought.

He wasn't particularly thirsty either, but he forced himself to drink most of the water so he wouldn't get dehydrated.

Since he wasn't going to eat it anyway, he thought maybe giving it to Oscar might win him a few points. "Do you want my food?" he asked as pleasantly as he could manage.

Oscar stared blankly at him.

"Give me your bowl, and I'll put mine in and give it back to you." Jeff wanted to hang onto his own bowl. He was afraid that if he lost his bowl he wouldn't get anything tomorrow.

Continued silence.

Jeff scooped the food out and patted it into a ball. He decided to try to throw it into Oscar's bowl. He made a few underhand swings to try to line up the shot.

Oscar's eyes were locked on the lump of food.

Jeff tossed it gently toward the bowl but missed by about a foot. The food splatted with a sickening sound on the floor that was filthy with Oscar's feces. Jeff cringed at the thought of eating food off of that floor, but it didn't seem to slow Oscar down at all. He scooped it off the floor and began shoving it into his mouth with both hands.

Jeff put his bowls by the slot in the door and went back to the mat.

He tried to keep his brain occupied. *Maybe I can actually make some use of this time*, he thought. *I really haven't had much time to think since I've been here. Everything's been happening so fast.*

He began to think about those strange 'feelings' he had been having that seemed to give him insight into other's thoughts. *Are they legitimate, or am I just imagining them?* he wondered.

They seemed to come in bursts. He had little control over them, and the more he concentrated on trying to understand what he was sensing, the less he was able to sense. It was as if he saw something out of the corner of his eye that disappeared if he tried to look directly at it.

Maybe I'm just imagining all of it, he thought. *Or maybe my mind is just interpreting non-verbal clues – a raised eyebrow, a sweaty upper lip – the way everyone does to some extent.*

He tried to think if there were any times that his feelings had been clearly proven insightful, but he couldn't think of any.

Then he realized that there was something unexplainable about the pheerion. He had clearly seen the pheerion in his dreams before he had even arrived... *didn't I?*

As he thought about it, he realized it wasn't all that clear. *Did I really see the pheerion, or did I just have a sense of evil, and once I did see it, I overlaid that image on top of what I had been seeing? I did seem to be able to understand what the one on the TV was saying... what's with that?*

He wondered if that was related to the other 'feelings' he had been having. He seemed to sense strong emotions and non-verbal things people were communicating. *Does that sense allow me to clearly understand things people are trying to communicate in other languages?*

Jeff shook his head. The more he thought about it,

the crazier it seemed. *As long as I'm thinking crazy things, maybe I should consider the possibility that I could be 'The Raja'.* Jeff laughed at that one.

He started to wonder if the whole thing was a dream. *Maybe when I 'went through the portal' I was really just scrambling my brain, and right now I'm lying in a hospital bed in some sort of coma with mom sitting there – crying.*

He shuddered at the thought of that.

No, this all seems too real – none of the strange ambiguity and confused, fluid nature of a dream.

There was a sudden noise that snapped Jeff out of his thoughts and made him jump.

Oscar snarled and lurched at the ends of his chains. He had quietly eased over as close as his chains would allow and then LUNGED, growling, at Jeff.

The panic started to set in again.

Chapter 37:

Jeff looked around at the interior of the wooden ship. He actually knew he was dreaming this time, so he wasn't as afraid as he had been. He decided he was going to stay with it this time and find out what happens next.

He had decided that these were more than simple dreams. He was convinced that he *had* clearly seen the pheerion before he even knew what one was. He had a feeling that his dreams were important, and he might be able to learn something if he paid attention.

The pheerion was there, and once again, he began to speak: *"You can't stop me boy!"*

At this point he usually woke up, but he was determined to stick with it.

"Not while I have the power of the artifact."

Jeff flinched as the pheerion raised his hand to strike, but the punch never came. Jeff looked and realized the pheerion was holding something in his raised hand.

Everything seemed to be moving in slow motion. Jeff zoomed in and saw the pheerion was holding...

His locket?

Jeff wondered what that meant, but as he watched the locket rotate, it was almost as if there was a voice in his head saying: 'Wait for it, wait for it...'

As the locket rotated... slowly... slowly... Jeff focused in on it, and it completely filled his view.

It had nearly rotated all the way around, and he expected to see his father's photo.

He didn't.

Instead, he saw *his own* face looking back at him.

Not me now. I'm much younger.

My father's locket!

Jeff woke up.

He was absolutely sure – at that moment – that the

dream was real, and it meant that the pheerion had contact with his father.

Jeff's heart was pounding. *My father is here! Somewhere. I know it!*

Don't I?

He looked around and remembered where he was. Oscar was snoring in his corner. As Jeff remembered his situation, the optimism began to fade. *Even if my father is here, how can I find him now?*

I'm stuck in this awful cell, and even if I could get out, what would I do? Tap the pheerion on the shoulder and say: 'Excuse me Mr. Lizard Creature, but I notice you have my father's locket. Would you mind telling me where you found that?'

Then he even started to wonder how *real* the dream even was. *For a moment, I was absolutely sure it was showing me something real, but that's ridiculous... Isn't it? Why would I even think that? It was just a dream. Am I going crazy?*

The panic he had felt was giving way to depression. His emotions just seemed to be all over the place.

Then he noticed something that brought the panic back – bigger and better than ever.

Jeff saw that, for some reason, Oscar's chains were no longer attached to his hands and wrists. They were on the floor, open, beside him.

Chapter 38:

Crap!

After seeing how Oscar had been acting the day before, Jeff was scared... *scared as hell...* to be trapped in the same cell with him with no shackles to hold him back.

Jeff HAD to somehow get him back in the shackles.

Jeff moved, slowly, cautiously, toward him. He tried to avoid stepping in the piles of feces but soon realized that was hopeless and a relatively minor concern at that moment.

He carefully lifted one of the shackles. The lock was missing. *How is that possible?!?!?* Jeff found one of the locks a few feet away. It was similar to a padlock. It was locked but not on the shackle and couldn't be opened without a key.

Hell!

Jeff looked around and saw another closed lock.

Somebody had to have done this. It couldn't have just 'happened'.

He had to find *some way* out.

He looked around the cell desperately. He checked the door which was solidly secured. *What chance do I have?* he thought. *People must spend years trying to get out of these cells. How can I hope to get out in hours?*

He felt around the back walls for any openings or weaknesses, but the stones were large and solid.

He scratched at the mortar between the stones and found it crumbled and fell away relatively easily. He ran his thumb around one of the stones, and he could see dust falling off the mortar.

Could it be that easy? he wondered. He shook his head. *Even if I could scrape the mortar away, these stones are huge. I could probably never budge one.*

The stones were each about two-feet by two-feet, and he had no idea how deep they were.

He looked around for some sort of tool, but there wasn't much in the cell. He tried to see if there was anything he could pull off the toilet, but it seemed secure. He thought about the shackles, but they were still securely chained.

There didn't seem to be anything he could use.

He saw the long spoon in the bowl. It was plastic but a fairly hard plastic. *Harder than my skin, and my thumb was enough to loosen the mortar.* He pulled it out of the bowl and tapped it against his hand. *It might be worth a try.*

He headed back to the wall with the spoon in hand. As he passed by Oscar, he heard him stir.

Jeff froze.

He watched as Oscar lifted his head, scratched the back of his neck...

Jeff tensed as Oscar rose...

Then rolled over and seemed to be right back asleep.

Jeff exhaled but didn't move for a few more minutes.

When it seemed clear that Oscar was back asleep, Jeff continued to the stone he had been on the rear wall.

He scraped the handle of the spoon around the stone and saw a satisfying shower of mortar dust falling to the floor. He rubbed for several more minutes, paused to admire the progress, then went back at it harder and faster.

He was definitely removing some of the mortar, but it would take a long time. *How deep are these stones? One-foot? Two-feet?*

The spoon's handle was only about ten inches, and even if he was able – somehow – to get all the way through, he still assumed the stone would be too heavy to move. He tried to push those doubts out of his mind. He didn't really have many options, and as hopeless as it seemed, there was something in the back of his mind telling him he was on the right track.

Probably just crazy delusions, but crazy delusions are more comforting than empty fear.

After about an hour, Jeff had dug an approximately one-inch groove all the way around the stone.

Impressive progress but nowhere near where he needed to be.

Every few minutes, he would pause when he heard Oscar stirring and watch for any signs of movement.

His arm and shoulder were aching. He dropped the spoon and rubbed his shoulder.

This is hopeless, he thought.

On a whim, he decided to push on the rock just to see what it felt like.

He braced his foot against an irregular stone in the floor that stuck up a couple inches. He put his hands firmly on the stone, got a good foothold on the rough, rocky floor, pushed with his leg, pushed with his arms and...

It didn't move even the slightest bit.

Not really surprising but still frustrating.

Oscar was stirring again. He seemed to be moving more frequently, and Jeff wondered if he was beginning to wake up.

He braced himself and pushed again, but again, the stone was clearly going nowhere.

He turned and sat. He watched Oscar and was afraid he could definitely see signs of waking.

He got back in position and pushed with everything he had...

And...

That time...

It moved!

Only a fraction of a millimeter at most, but there was no doubt in Jeff's mind that he felt it *move*... as crazy as that seemed.

He re-braced himself and pushed again...

It moved a little more.

Not much, but it was moving.

He continued to push, and it seemed to be getting a little easier. It felt like he was getting stronger as he went. He had a strange sensation in his muscles – as if there was some extra energy being pumped into them, like adrenalin but stronger.

He had moved it about six inches, but he was completely worn out. He sat and rested and watched Oscar.

His heart leapt as he realized as he saw one of Oscar's eyes glinting back at him.

He turned around and pushed with everything he had. The stone continued to slowly slide. Jeff didn't stop to think that what he was doing was *completely impossible*, he just kept going.

He looked over his shoulder and saw Oscar beginning to move toward him.

The stone moved a little bit, and Oscar moved a little bit, the stone moved some more, and Oscar moved some more.

The stone had moved more than a foot, and it was still going. It seemed to go a little faster and a little easier as he went, but he couldn't see any daylight yet.

Then he felt something on his ankle. Oscar had grabbed his ankle in an iron grip. Jeff looked around startled, and at that same moment, he felt the stone fall away. He had been pushing so hard that he fell through the hole he had just created. While his legs were still back in the cell, his body was hanging out of the hole, and the mass of his body pulled his legs – with Oscar still hanging on – through the hole and over the edge.

He found himself dangling by his ankle 200 feet in the air.

Jeff hadn't really thought about the fact that his cell likely wasn't on the ground floor – they had taken an elevator to get to it, after all. In fact, he had been so focused on getting through that he hadn't spent a lot of time speculating what would happen after he got through.

He had figured that was just a detail he would have to deal with when he got to that point.

He was at that point.

He was hanging 200 feet in the air, and the only thing preventing him from falling to his death was a maniac who would surely dismember him as soon as he could haul him back up.

Jeff flailed wildly – more out of desperation and instinct than any plan or common sense.

He felt Oscar's grip begin to slip but then felt another hand slapping and grabbing at him. It seemed that Oscar wasn't going to give up his prize easily. Oscar's hands were grabbing so violently that Jeff was bleeding, and that blood was making it hard for Oscar to maintain his hold.

Jeff felt himself starting to slide out of Oscar's grasp. Oscar was halfway out of the hole, and it seemed he might follow Jeff down rather than relinquish him.

Jeff was sliding out of Oscar's grasp. He took a look over his shoulder and saw the disappointed look on his former cell-mates face as he began to fall.

This was it.

Within a few seconds, he'd be dead.

Chapter 39:

He hit the ground much sooner than he thought he would, and it was much softer and less violent an impact than he would have imagined. He saw Baldwin's face and heard Nahima's voice saying: "Well this is getting to be a habit."

Jeff was in Artimus' car. Artimus was driving, Nahima was in the front passenger seat, and Baldwin was in the rear with Jeff. It was still dark. It had seemed an eternity since the day before, and Jeff had imagined they were well into morning. But the sun hadn't even come up yet.

"ARE YOU OKAY?" Artimus had to shout so that his voice could be heard over the wind noise.

Jeff nodded. "I THINK SO."

"STRAP IN AND HOLD ON. THINGS MIGHT GET ROUGH HERE. WE CAN TALK WHEN WE'VE HAD A CHANCE TO SETTLE DOWN."

Jeff reached for his seat-belt and was trying to connect it when Artimus hit the accelerator, and they took off so fast that Jeff's arms were plastered against the seat before he could finish connecting.

Jeff looked over his shoulder and realized there were two flying police-cars in hot pursuit.

Green energy bolts flashed past as Artimus' car rocked, zig-zagged and bounced violently. Artimus was trying to make them as difficult to hit as possible.

Jeff managed to get his seat-belt fastened and found a strange, relieved peace as they rocketed at 200 mph weaving between buildings while the police shot at them.

It all felt much safer than where he had been.

Artimus was weaving frantically back and forth and up and down to try to avoid the energy bolts that seemed to be coming from all directions. Jeff bounced and slid and shook in his seat, but all the moves were so quick that he never went too far in any one direction.

Artimus was fiddling with some knobs and didn't seem to see the large building directly in their path.

"Dad," Nahima said gently. She touched him on the arm and pointed at the looming building.

Jeff was about to shout a much more urgent warning with far more exclamation points for emphasis, but Artimus looked up, yanked on the yoke, and they veered around the building just in time.

Jeff looked back to see how the police cars would react. One turned the other way and disappeared from view, but the other one stayed right with them. Green flashes continued to zip past. Jeff could hear the sounds of the closer ones. They gave off a low frequency hum that rumbled his insides even when they didn't contact.

Before Jeff could take much comfort in the police car they lost, two more joined the pursuit. Jeff realized, with some discomfort, that the density of fire was increasing and it seemed inevitable that eventually one would make solid contact.

Shortly after Jeff had that thought, they did suffer a glancing hit on Baldwin's side. Baldwin jumped and let out a startled yelp as the vehicle rocked violently.

"That's not good." Artimus glanced at various dials and indicators as he increased speed.

They were going very fast with barely enough time to dodge each new building as it approached. It seemed Artimus felt it was better to take his chances with greater speed and faith in his own flying skills rather than making himself an easier target for the police guns.

They began to open up some more distance between themselves and the three vehicles that were still in pursuit.

I wonder why he doesn't get up and out of these buildings... I guess we'd be too much in the open then and easier targets...

Jeff caught his breath as a fourth police car showed up – headed straight at them in a near head-on collision course. Its guns fired furiously as it approached with frightening speed.

Artimus held his course and won the game of 'chicken' against the new arrival. The police vehicle veered off and ended up in a position that would make it difficult for him to turn and catch up with the others.

Jeff saw that they were approaching the edge of the city, and the houses in front of them were much smaller and sparser than the large, city buildings. Jeff found himself facing conflicting feelings of relief and concern. Relief that they'd no longer have to dodge buildings but concern they'd be easier targets for the police.

As they passed the edge of the city and the last of the big buildings, Artimus pulled the lever – which Jeff had come to recognize as the throttle – ALL the way back.

Artimus' car was FAST.

They shot forward with a speed that Jeff would have had a hard time imagining if he hadn't been actually experiencing it.

"SORRY, I CAN'T PUT THE TOP UP AT THIS SPEED. HANG ON FOR A FEW MORE MINUTES, AND THEN WE'LL HAVE A CHANCE TO TALK," Artimus explained.

Jeff tried to turn his head to get a look at the police cars. The wind and acceleration made even simple movements difficult. Jeff thought he saw the police falling back, but he couldn't be sure.

Jeff thought he could see the blue force screen that surrounded Caesurmia in the distance, and they were closing fast.

"HANG ON EVERYBODY. THE POLICE WILL HAVE LOCKED THE SCREEN," Artimus said. He pulled on his controls, and they began to climb almost straight up. Jeff felt himself pushing deep, deep into his seat.

The screen seemed to go forever. Jeff's ears popped, and he was finding it hard to breath. They crested the top

edge of the screen, and Artimus began to bring them down
– at a more leisurely pace.

"OKAY, THEY SHOULDN'T FOLLOW US
BEYOND THE BARRIER. ONCE I'VE PUT A
LITTLE MORE DISTANCE BETWEEN US, WE'LL
SET DOWN. CONGRATULATIONS EVERYBODY,
WE ARE NOW OFFICIALLY FUGITIVES."

Chapter 40:

Fugitives?

While Jeff was absolutely ecstatic to be out of that prison cell, the thought that he had turned his new friends – who had taken him in and treated him with such kindness, not to mention twice saving his life – into *fugitives* was not sitting well with him at all.

They had been flying for about fifteen minutes over seemingly endless forest, and the sun was just coming up. Artimus found an opening and brought the car down. The area was washed with a subtle orange glow as the sun was just starting to show over the horizon.

"Look, I'm sorry," Jeff blurted out as soon as it was quiet enough to easily talk.

"You're sorry?" Artimus asked.

"You know... about getting all of you into trouble... turning you all into fugitives."

Artimus smiled. "That's not your fault. We knew what we were doing. With or without you, we needed to get out... to do something. Doclotnury needs our help. If our government doesn't have the... courage to act, we have to see what we can do. Besides, I'm the one who got you in trouble, remember?"

Jeff flushed. He had been annoyed with Artimus for hanging him out there, but that seemed ancient history. "So what do we do now?"

"A friend of mine, an old war buddy named Dave Kimble, lives in the forest but closer to Doclotnury. I haven't talked to him for a while. He's not big on electro-comm devices, but he's a good guy. I'm sure he'll put us up and help us out. We *should* have enough power to get there."

Jeff wasn't sure if he liked the emphasis Artimus put on the word 'should'.

"He's a little... I'm not sure if 'crazy' is too indelicate a word, but that's what he is." Artimus caught Jeff's concerned look. "But don't get me wrong, he's the greatest guy in the world. He'd give his life to help a friend without even thinking.

"Anyway, we should have enough power to make it to his place. It'll take about..." Artimus looked at his watch. "Three hours to get there."

Jeff did some quick math in his head and figured that would be about seven and a half Earth hours.

"Once we meet up with Dave," Artimus continued, "we'll head toward Doclotnury and see how we can help. It seems that General Rasp, the pheerion warlord, is leading an attack fleet toward Doclotnury. I've been hearing some preliminary reports that sound grim. Things seem to be getting ugly very quickly.

"The pheerions have ancient technology compared to humans. While they've always tended to be violent and warring, they've never tried anything this ambitious. They use potassium nitrate-powder cannons and pistols, wooden sailing ships..."

The mention of 'wooden sailing ships' struck a chord with Jeff.

"No real match for modern technology, but it seems they've obtained some secret weapons – they have a modern force shield and some sort of huge energy cannon... well you saw that video. That could make them a real threat.

"The Doclotnurians have been launching attacks against their fleet as it's on the move, but they can't penetrate the energy shield. I'm not sure what we can do, but I'd like to go and offer any assistance we can."

Some shadows passed over them, and Jeff looked apprehensively toward the sky. He saw several of the huge badger-headed bird-creatures that he had seen shortly after arriving.

"Oh, don't worry about them," Artimus said after

seeing the fear in Jeff's eyes. "They won't come after us unless we appear sick or wounded."

With that said, Artimus pushed a button that raised the roof. Apparently he wasn't as sure as he sounded.

"So fill us in on you," Artimus said. "I hope things weren't too difficult for you."

Jeff cringed. He didn't want to be a whiner, but *yes things were pretty friggin' difficult for me.* Instead of being that blunt he said: "Well, first off, that Duanan is a complete ass."

"I think he's been under a lot of pressure since the start of the pheerion offensive," Artimus said.

Jeff didn't bother to argue or offer any details, but he did say: "I think someone tried to kill me."

Artimus' eyes widened. "What?!?!"

"They put me in a cell with some sort of... violent maniac."

Artimus looked concerned but remained silent as Jeff explained.

"He was chained up last night, but when I woke up, his chains were unlocked. It seems *someone* must have snuck in when we were both sleeping and freed him so he could kill me, and it would look like an accident."

Artimus still didn't speak but looked very concerned and thoughtful.

"How did you get through that wall?" Baldwin asked excitedly.

Jeff shrugged. "I just spent some time digging at the mortar, then pushed at the rock. I'm a little surprised myself that I was able to move it, but I did."

Jeff realized that all three sets of eyes were focused on him intently.

"Those stones are huge!" Baldwin said, breaking the silence after a few moments. "I don't... I don't think I could even move one of those."

Jeff shrugged again. He didn't know what else to say. He was surprised when it moved also, but it did and that was that. "I think my father is here somewhere."

Again he had all six eyes focused intently on him. "I've been having these... dreams... of a pheerion. I think it may be... General Rasp? I started having the dreams before I even got here, and I think they're... telling me something. I had one last night, and it was very clear, and the pheerion was holding my father's locket. One with *MY* photo in it."

As the words came out of his mouth, Jeff suddenly realized he was a lot less convinced than he had been a short time ago. When he had just woken, he felt the dream was very important, but now – just as they didn't seem as frightening in the light of day – they also seemed less believable.

"Where is your locket?"

"Last I saw it, Duanan had it in his desk drawer."

Again Artimus seemed to be concerned and thoughtful.

"I have a question," Jeff said. "How did you know where and when to find me at exactly the right time?"

"Well the 'where' is simple." Artimus held up the electronic tracker programmed to track the marker on Jeff's tooth. "As for the 'when'... well Nahima just had a 'feeling' that we should head out when we did, and... well, that feeling paid off, didn't it?"

"You should know by now not to doubt me," Nahima said grinning.

"Well let's see if we can do something to help the Doclotnurians, and hopefully, find your father in the process," Artimus said as he started the car and eased it off the ground.

Chapter 41:

The scenery was spectacular, but Jeff was beginning to get restless. His seat was comfortable, but he wasn't used to traveling that distance without at least being able to get up and stretch his legs.

He also wasn't used to seeing so much land that hadn't been paved, mined or dammed. He had seen a few scattered human 'villages', and there were some long paths that had been cleared of trees. He assumed those paths were what passed for 'roads'. There were a number of interesting and unusual animals, but Jeff was too high up to get as good a look as he would have liked. The ones that seemed most plentiful were herds of deer-like animals that he saw grazing in a number of different clearings.

They saw great forests, plains, streams and waterfalls. Jeff felt privileged and almost embarrassed that he was getting a chance to see such unspoiled land. It was almost like being with Lewis and Clark but without having to actually paddle the canoe or deal with the other difficulties they had to endure. He was able to just soar over all of it and view the splendor in pampered comfort.

"Oh, here." Baldwin fished under his seat and pulled out a gun-belt. "I almost forgot. I modified it just for you." He reached down again and lifted Jeff's baseball bat. He put it through a special loop on the belt and handed it to Jeff.

"Cool! Thanks!" Jeff said.

He turned the belt and gun over in his lap examining it closely. Under normal circumstances, he would have been absolutely thrilled to have such a device to call his own.

As it was though, it was a reminder.

It wasn't just a toy but something that he might need to defend himself from some absolutely horrifying creatures.

He thought it was funny that Baldwin seemed to think the bat was so important. Jeff had only grabbed it because it was the closest, easiest thing he could think of. Nothing like the gun he had now.

Still... without the bat, I would have been dead when that snake thing came after me, so it did save my life.

He patted it appreciatively as he thought of that.

"You don't know where you're going, do you?" Nahima teasingly asked Artimus.

"Oh, we're almost there. We should be able to see it any minute..."

At that moment, the car *lurched* downward and then stabilized at a lower level.

"We're... uhhhh... we're running a little low on energy." Artimus explained.

The car lurched down again, and this time rather than leveling off, Artimus pointed the nose down and toward a clearing that was visible but a few miles away.

"What about your reserve?" Nahima asked.

"I started using the reserve about ten minutes ago," Artimus said a bit sheepishly. "I figured that would leave us plenty to get there."

Jeff's knuckles turned white as his hands clenched his seat-belt. They were moving fast. Artimus seemed to still have control, and he seemed to be trying to get them into the clearing rather than putting efforts into reducing speed. Jeff wasn't sure what good it would do to hit a clearing if they were going 400 mph.

Jeff tended to only be religious when it was convenient, and he found it very convenient at that moment. He was praying frantically, squeezing his seat-belt and sweating.

He glanced at Baldwin who seemed nervous but not as bad as Jeff would have imagined. Baldwin had seemed somewhat timid prior to that, but he seemed more composed than Jeff at that moment.

Jeff closed his eyes and concentrated on his breathing. He hadn't really had the time or presence of mind to think much about the fact that he was going to die when he was fighting the snake or hanging out of the hole in the jail wall.

Now that he was hurtling toward his death and had time to think about it, he was disappointed to find that it was a lot like *not* hurtling toward his death – only with a hell of a lot more fear thrown in.

He would have hoped that it would have been more poetic than that.

The ground was coming up... *fast*.

When they had been higher up, Jeff really didn't have a good sense of how fast they were going, but now that they were closer to the ground, the treetops were becoming a sickening greenish-brown blur.

Jeff saw some sort of movement out of the corner of his eye, and then he felt his spine compress as his stomach went from his throat to his ass.

He looked up, and through a glass panel in the roof of the car, he could see a parachute deployed above them.

I guess it would make sense to have a safety parachute in flying cars, he thought to himself.

He tried to compose himself before anyone else noticed how nervous he had been.

"Everybody hang on. I think we're clear," Artimus said as they eased into the clearing.

After several more tense moments, they made a jarring landing.

"Everybody okay?" Artimus asked.

After determining that nobody had been hurt, they climbed out and gathered at the rear of the car to collect their supplies.

"It's going to be a bit of a walk," Artimus said as he surveyed the terrain, "but it shouldn't be too bad."

He buckled a gun-belt around his waist and slung a battered bag over his shoulder. He paused and seemed to studying their location very intently and calculating some details in his mind. "We should have at least another hour of daylight, and that should give us plenty of time."

Jeff buckled his gun-belt and looked around. The clearing was only a few hundred yards in diameter, and they were surrounded by trees. After Jeff's experience right after he had arrived, he wasn't very anxious to have to go through the woods on foot. He wanted to raise the subject but also didn't want tip everybody off regarding just how nervous he was.

"Are there any ... roads... or anything we can take?" Jeff asked as coolly as he could manage.

Artimus shook his head. "We may be able to find some paths. Dave has cleared some trails and areas, but mostly we'll probably be cutting through trees and brush."

Artimus began walking with long strides and a brisk pace while the others did their best to keep up. He seemed to recognize that Jeff was nervous. "There are some dangerous animals out here, but keep your wits about you. If we're cautious, we shouldn't have any problems. Make plenty of noise so we don't take anything by surprise. If anything takes us by surprise, well..." Artimus paused as he scanned the tree line just ahead of them. "We'll just have to deal with that as necessary."

When they arrived at the tree line, Artimus stopped and drew his gun. The others did the same.

Then they crossed the threshold.

Chapter 42:

"Keep your safeties on. If you shoot, make damn sure you know what you're shooting at before you pull the trigger. Not only will that help to make sure none of us get shot, but there are some things around here... well let's just say that if you shoot them, you probably won't hurt them – just piss them off."

After his last comment, Artimus looked at Jeff who was cringing. He lowered his voice a bit as he addressed Jeff directly: "Sorry. Don't want to scare you, but I do want you to be prepared."

Artimus slowed down as they came to some heavy brush. He holstered his weapon and pushed the tall weeds out of the way. The others followed him single file. Jeff, then Baldwin, and Nahima brought up the rear. The rest of them kept their guns drawn.

After about five minutes they had made their way through that particularly thick patch, and Artimus drew his weapon again.

"Just keep your eyes open." He scanned left to right as they walked.

Jeff looked up. He remembered the blob-like thing that had fallen out of the tree. "Uhhh…" He looked at Artimus. "When I first got here, I saw some shapeless... *thing*... fall out of a tree."

"Ah... a jelly-wart. Don't worry about them. They're not very common and won't attack anything as big as us – particularly if we keep moving. If one hits you, try to shake it off as quickly as possible before it gets a chance to do too much damage."

Jeff noticed that Artimus had assured him they wouldn't attack, before offering advice for what to do if one *did* attack.

Jeff cut to the bottom line in his mind: *So yes, one*

might attack.
  He took another quick look up.

Chapter 43:

They had been walking for about two of Jeff's hours (less than one of Artimus' hours), and Jeff was starting to relax and enjoy himself. The largest animals they'd seen had been some squirrel-like rodents. They had also seen a few lizards and birds but nothing that seemed to present a threat.

The sounds of the forest were becoming hypnotic. The rhythmic chirping of birds and insects blended with crunching of the four sets of human feet on soft dirt and twigs along with the sound of Artimus' humming – which he had been doing to keep some noise going whenever he didn't have enough to say.

Jeff froze.

Baldwin bumped into him, and Artimus turned when he sensed something was going on. Then he also stopped.

Jeff held up a hand and looked around. He had a strong sense of *something*, and he wanted a moment of silence to see if he could hear anything.

"Something's not right," he said after about ten seconds.

The four of them scanned their surroundings.

"I don't hear any birds," Artimus said.

Jeff realized that, yes, there was an unusual lack of bird sounds which they had heard steadily ever since they had entered the forest.

They continued standing and listening for a while but couldn't sense anything else unusual.

"Well... I don't see or hear anything. Should we continue?" Artimus asked.

"I guess so," Jeff said.

Artimus began walking again, and after about six steps, Jeff saw a brief glimpse of a shadowy movement. "Hold it," he said quietly but with urgency.

Jeff pointed to some movement he saw through the trees approximately one-hundred feet away.

It was something big.

All four of them readied their guns and took positions that would ensure they wouldn't hit each other if they had to fire.

They were all looking in the direction of the movement, but whatever it was had stopped and they couldn't see anything except trees and other vegetation.

Jeff squinted. He knew there was something there, but he couldn't distinguish anything.

Then he saw it!

Through the trees, he could see something that looked similar to a HUGE praying mantis – about eight feet tall – but with some differences. Its head was proportionately larger than a scaled up mantis head would have been, and there were some other differences in its shape and proportions. It also had a rough, mottled-brown exoskeleton as opposed to the green of the ones Jeff had seen in his mother's gardens. The color and texture gave it the appearance of a tree, and Jeff realized that's why they didn't see it clearly until it started to move. Jeff hastily dialed his gun to 10.

Artimus fired, and that was the cue the others had been waiting for. All four opened fire, but the shots seemed to just hit the exoskeleton without doing much more than slightly annoying it.

"Run for it!" Artimus shouted, and the four of them took off in a panic.

I guess this is one of the ones that just gets pissed off, Jeff thought to himself, realizing that Artimus hadn't followed his own advice.

Artimus let the others get ahead of him, and he fired a few shots over his shoulder as he brought up the rear.

The mantis seemed to be able to run at roughly the same speed as the humans, so they were able to maintain some distance.

Can it fly? Jeff wondered.

If so, it wasn't taking advantage of that ability... yet.

The four continued to run. Nahima led, Jeff was right behind her, then Baldwin then Artimus.

Jeff was acting on pure adrenalin. His legs were moving, but he could hardly feel them. It was as if he is body was floating and moving very fast through the forest.

Jeff glanced over his shoulder. He could still see the mantis, but they were keeping a good distance.

Jeff hoped it might decide this meal wasn't worth the trouble... soon.

The pain in his throat and lungs was beginning to overwhelm the adrenaline, and he wasn't moving nearly as smoothly as he had originally.

From the rear, Artimus stumbled. He continued off balance for several steps but then hit the ground hard.

Baldwin was the first to notice something wasn't right. "Dad?".

Baldwin stopped, hesitated for a moment not quite sure what to do. Then he headed back for his father.

Jeff and Nahima had continued for fifty yards before realizing something was wrong. Jeff looked over his shoulder, and when he realized Baldwin wasn't right there, he stopped and shouted to Nahima.

She turned, and the two of them headed back toward Baldwin who was crouched by Artimus and firing wildly toward the mantis – which seemed to be momentarily mesmerized and had stopped moving.

Nahima fired a couple shots as she ran but the long range, and the unsteadiness of her running shots sent the energy bolts flying far off-target. "Shoot for the eyes!" Nahima shouted.

Baldwin shot two rounds toward the mantis' head, but neither made contact. He paused and tried to relax.

The mantis was moving again and was within approximately twenty feet when Baldwin fired again.

That one connected!

A direct hit to the creature's left eye that left a black, smoldering hole.

The mantis stood for a few moments.

And then it fell.

It hit the ground with a loud, ground-shaking thud. It was deceptively heavy. Its body shape was lean which gave it the visual illusion of being light, but it was large enough to have some serious mass.

Yes!

Nahima and Jeff shouted for joy. Baldwin just stared speechless and then turned his attention to Artimus who was moving groggily. "Dad! Dad, are you okay."

"I think so," Artimus said, rubbing his head. "What happened?"

Baldwin hugged him as he sat up and said: "I got him! I got him!"

Artimus smiled.

Jeff had the feeling that the smile was less about the joy of surviving a deadly situation and more about the deeper fulfillment of seeing Baldwin so happy and proud.

Nahima and Jeff patted Baldwin on the back.

"That was great! You're a hero," Nahima said as Baldwin beamed.

Chapter 44:

It had taken quite a while for everyone to regain their breath, but they were soon back on their way.

As they walked, Artimus assured them that they were nearly there, but Jeff was nervously noting how quickly the sun was approaching the horizon. He also noticed that Artimus had been telling them they were 'almost there' for quite some time.

Jeff also noticed, with some discomfort, that Artimus' assurances seemed to belie his own uncertainty. Artimus was checking the position of the sun frequently – too frequently for it to have moved much from the last check. It seemed to have become something of a nervous habit.

Jeff could see a large, impressive cliff wall rising ahead of them. They reached the edge of the tree-line and saw there was a dry creek bed that ran along the base of the cliff.

Artimus paused, looked left then right and seemed to be thinking.

Jeff was hyper-aware of any uncertainty Artimus seemed to be experiencing, and he didn't like the pause.

"Good, we're almost there," Artimus said cheerily after a nerve-wracking few moments. "About a ten to twenty minute walk up this creek-bed, and we should be there." He pointed to the right.

The four continued with some renewed energy. Jeff eyed the sun nervously. He wasn't thrilled about being in the forest in the day-light. The thought of being out there at night... *I don't... I can't... the stress of the last couple days is just getting to be too much.*

Jeff felt a wave of panic wash over him. His hand squeezed tight around the grip of his gun, and he felt the sweat of his palm making the rubbery grip slick.

Ahead of them, the creek bed took a sharp bend to

the left. As they arrived at the bend, the four of them stopped suddenly.

A huge, black animal rose from behind a large boulder about fifty feet ahead of them. It was seven or eight feet tall, broad, heavy and powerfully built.

Jeff's first thought was that it was a grizzly, but then he realized that, while its head, body shape, size and fur were all bear-like, it had arms, legs, feet and *hands* that all seemed more human – or at least gorilla.

"A brune," Baldwin said in a loud whisper.

The beast growled threateningly, and four guns snapped into position.

Jeff could feel his heart pounding, and while he was trying to keep the beast steadily sighted, he was finding it hard to keep the gun from shaking.

The brune roared – a much more threatening vocalization than before – and its fur stood up, making it appear even larger than before.

It was something of a stand-off. None of the humans wanted to shoot such a magnificent animal just for being there, but no one wanted to be dismembered either. Then there was that: *'you might just piss it off'* to consider as well.

While the creature was bulky, Jeff could see the muscle mass beneath that bulk and suspected it could move very quickly in short bursts.

It growled again.

Wait!

Jeff lowered his gun slowly and studied the face of the brune.

Artimus saw Jeff lowering his gun, and while he tried to remain focused on the brune, he was distracted by Jeff. "Jeff?"

The last time the brune had roared, Jeff had heard a very clear voice in his head that said: *'I'm scared.'*

It was similar to what he heard when the pheerion spoke – a sort of simultaneous translation.

"Wait!" Jeff said as he raised a hand and stepped a

little ahead of the others. He put his gun in its holster.

"It's just scared. I think I may be able to... communicate ... with it."

Jeff was nearly as surprised as the others to hear those words come out of his mouth, but he had a strong feeling he should try to deal with the situation that way.

He took a few cautious steps forward and said: "Can you understand me?"

The brune made a low grumbling noise that Jeff could understand was a puzzled '*Yes*'.

"We don't want to hurt you. We were just walking through. We surprised you, and you surprised us."

The brune growled again, and Jeff understood something like: '*Not hurt. Scared. Don't hurt.*'

Jeff was having some trouble understanding. He thought that the reason it was so hard to understand was that the brune, while very intelligent for an animal, probably had a language that was very simple compared to his.

He wasn't sure if the brune was saying he wouldn't hurt them, or that he didn't want them to hurt him, but either way, it seemed as long as they had some understanding of each other, nobody would get hurt.

"We just need to get past," Jeff said. He took some slow, measured steps forward and toward the tree line to show that they would take a wide path and give the brune plenty of room.

The other three stood where they were, unsure of what, exactly, was going on. Jeff wanted to make sure it was going to work before telling them to follow. He was just at the edge of the trees.

"See, we don't want to hurt you."

He was about to tell the others to walk slowly toward him, but before he had a chance, there was a loud crashing sound behind him.

Before Jeff had any idea what was happening, he felt searing pain in his stomach and back. His vision went blurry from the pain, and his view of the landscape shifted as his body rose and tilted.

The mantis was apparently not as dead as they had assumed, and Jeff was firmly in its grasp. There were spikes on its 'arms' that were piercing Jeff's flesh.

Jeff felt like he was going to pass out, and he found it hard to concentrate or focus his eyes. Then he saw a large shadow fill his field of view.

The next thing Jeff knew, he was on the ground. He could see and *hear* the brune grappling with the mantis.

The animals clashed with a frightening power, and the ground shook as the two massive creatures battled with intense ferocity.

Jeff interpreted the brune's current roars as angry – VERY angry with a little fear thrown in.

Angry because the mantis attacked me? Jeff wondered.

Jeff was regaining his senses. His shirt was stained with blood, and while it still hurt, he felt that he was functional.

The others were tentatively moving forward – wanting to help Jeff but absolutely terrified of the battle between the two beasts which was thrashing, LOUD and violent.

Jeff rose shakily, and remembering how ineffective guns had been in the past, instead, reached for the baseball bat.

He took a firm grip on the bat, put it over his right shoulder and CHARGED.

He swung at the Mantis' leg and heard and felt a satisfying 'crack'.

The mantis faltered, but it had spare legs. It quickly regained its balance – though the brune was able to take advantage of the momentary distraction and gain a better position.

Jeff hit it again, this time in the body, and he could tell he was doing some damage. After a few more hits, the mantis seemed dazed, and Jeff worked alongside the brune to get it on the ground where Jeff was able to get an open shot at the head.

He raised the bat and brought it down as hard as he could.

The head cracked open, and yellow goo oozed out. The mantis twitched a bit, but there was no question that this time it was absolutely dead.

The brune sat heavily on the ground, and Jeff rushed to its side. "Are you all right?"

The animal growled, and Jeff got a jumble of thoughts: Pain, fear, relief, anger...

Affection?

Jeff had a strong sense that this animal cared about him. That's why it had risked its own life to save him.

But the brune had been badly hurt in the battle, and it slumped onto the ground.

The others rushed over.

"Are you okay?" Artimus asked nervously, eying the blood on his shirt.

"I'm not sure." Jeff felt dazed. The pain was nearly unbearable, and he felt like he was on the verge of blacking out. He could, periodically, see black spots, and he felt nauseous.

Artimus dug frantically in his bag for a first aid kit.

"Can you help him?" Jeff nodded toward the brune.

Artimus glanced over at the brune but was clearly more concerned with Jeff. "I'm going to inject you with a general painkiller." He pulled out a small hypodermic and injected it into Jeff's arm. "You may get drowsy. Don't fight it. Just relax."

He looked into the bag for some other supplies. "I'm going to inject each of the wound areas with a solution that will kill any bacteria and greatly speed healing. After that, I'll use these adhesive squares," he said as he held up some 4 inch by 4 inch squares. "To hold the wounds closed. Don't pull on the adhesive patches. They'll be bonded very strongly to your skin. After about four days, they should loosen and fall off by themselves, but if you get anxious…" He made a point to look Jeff in the eye to make sure he understood. "You'll tear the skin and re-open the wound. Let me know if you have any problems. I'll try to check them each day, but remind me in case I forget."

Jeff looked at Artimus. He was a little relieved that Artimus seemed to know what he was doing. "What about the brune?"

Artimus ignored the question and continued working on Jeff. "I'm not a doctor, but I have done this before. The wounds don't look too deep. I think you'll be all right. Just try to relax."

"What about the brune…" Jeff trailed off as he lost consciousness.

Chapter 45:

When Jeff woke he was in a dingy shack. He was lying on a worn and stained sofa.

He scanned the room. It looked like a home, but it was nothing like Artimus' house. There were pieces of mechanical... *junk* scattered around along with dirty glasses, dishes, and what looked like animal skins.

Jeff sat up. He rubbed his head. He had the most intense headache, and every muscle in his body ached. The wounds in his stomach and back also hurt but not as badly as he would have imagined. They felt like bad bruises. He rubbed his hand across his stomach and felt the patches.

While Jeff didn't feel like dancing a jig – actually he wasn't sure if he even knew what a 'jig' was – Artimus' medicines really seemed to dramatically speed healing.

The door began to creak open, and Jeff instinctively tensed. He had been through a lot in the last day or so and he found himself fearing what would happen next.

Artimus entered. "Jeff! You're up. How are you feeling?"

"Not bad," Jeff said and then cringed as a pain shot through his head. "How long was I out?"

"A couple hours. You were... relatively... fortunate. I don't think any of the punctures penetrated much beyond the muscle."

"What about the Brune?" Jeff asked.

Artimus smiled. "He's fine. It turns out he's a... friend... of Dave's." Artimus shook his head. "Leave it to Dave." He paused and looked at Jeff. "Or *you*... to befriend a brune." He shook his head again. "He's out in the yard with the others. I'm not real comfortable with it, but everybody else seems okay with him there..." He lowered his voice. "Brunes can be *savage* beasts. I've never heard of a tame one before.

"Come on outside – if you're feeling up to it – I'll introduce you to Dave."

Jeff followed Artimus out to a very large porch that looked out onto a spacious, dirt yard that was surrounded by a large, sturdy fence. It was dark.

Baldwin and Nahima were sitting on the porch as was the brune and a very large, unkempt man. Sitting to the left of the man was a huge... *dog? Wolf? Wolf-dog?*

Nahima and Baldwin nodded and smiled at Jeff as he passed. Artimus walked him toward the man who was using a large knife to shave pieces off of some sort of meat stick.

"Dave," Artimus said.

The man looked over his shoulder as he flicked a chunk of meat off his knife into his mouth.

"This is Jeff Browning," Artimus continued, "Jeff, this is Dave Kimble."

Jeff nodded. "Hello, nice to meet you."

"Mmmm," the man responded nodding. He was HUGE. Built like a defensive lineman. He patted a spot, between him and the brune with his right hand.

Jeff took that as an invitation – or request – to sit, and he complied. The brune reached over and patted Jeff forcefully on his shoulder. Jeff interpreted that as a sign of affection and smiled at him.

"Big Benji seems to like you," Dave said.

Jeff turned to face Dave and involuntarily flinched as his eyes met Dave's... crazy eyes... staring back at his.

"Benji don't like many people." He leaned in and lowered his voice. "'Tween you and me, I don't think he likes Artimus much." He grinned and popped another chunk of meat into his mouth. Then turned toward Artimus and winked.

Nahima stood up, stretched and brushed the dirt off the back of her pants.

"Whoa, Nahima, you're filling out nice," Dave said,

leering.

"You like it? Nahima asked. "You couldn't handle it." She said and smacked her butt.

Artimus was giving them both a very unpleasant look.

Dave nudged Jeff. "Look at Arty. Oh, we're just kidding, Arty. I'd thought you'd have learned to loosen up by now... *Bishop*."

He put a sarcastic twang on 'Bishop', and Jeff cringed. He was afraid Artimus – who already seemed to be getting a little annoyed – might lash out.

Artimus just laughed. "It really is good to see you again. You help me keep things in perspective."

Dave pulled his gun out of his holster, aimed at something near the fence and fired. Jeff saw the flash hit a small rodent.

"Go get it boy," Dave said and patted the wolf-dog on the shoulders.

The dog shot across the dirt yard. Jeff expected him to fetch the rodent and bring it back. Instead the dog sniffed at the rodent, circling it a few times, picked it up in his jaws, flipped his head back and swallowed the rodent down – bones and all – with a couple chomping bites.

Jeff cringed.

Dave turned his attention back to Jeff. "Artimus tells me he thinks you're 'The Raja'."

Jeff flushed. He wasn't sure how to respond.

Dave popped another chunk of meat into his mouth. "I don't believe it."

Jeff was prepared to say 'don't worry about it', expecting Dave to offer an apology for not believing it, but then he realized Dave wasn't offering any apologies.

"I met the Prophet once," Dave said matter-of-factly.

Jeff thought that was an interesting revelation.

"I thought she was full of plooch."

While Jeff still wasn't sure what to make of all these 'prophecies' and other things, he felt that the prophet may have some information that could help him find his father.

"Do you think you could introduce me to her... after all this war stuff is over?"

Dave looked at Jeff with an expression Jeff couldn't read. "She's sort of hard to get to... if she's not dead... but sure... I got nothing better to do... assuming you and I both live through all this... 'war stuff.'"

He grinned at Jeff... a toothy, creepy, leering grin.

Somewhere... deep in Jeff's brain... his neurons were wetting themselves from fear.

Chapter 46:

The next morning, Jeff woke to the wonderful smell of meat cooking. He had been sleeping on the sofa. Baldwin and Nahima looked like they had just woken. Jeff could see Artimus and Dave laughing outside. Jeff pressed on the patches that covered his wounds and was amazed to find the wounds beneath felt nearly healed.

"You ready for some breakfast?" Baldwin asked.

"Yeah, I'm starved." Jeff had been unconscious through dinner the night before and didn't really feel like eating anything when he did come to.

Jeff hopped off the sofa and headed outside with the other two.

Artimus and Dave were standing by some sort of fire pit.

As they got closer, Jeff saw that there were several gutted rodents on a spit. They were the size of squirrels... or rats.

He looked at Baldwin who had an unpleasant expression on his face. The expression was similar to the look of someone who had just seen his breakfast and realized it consisted of gutted rodents on a spit.

"Good morning! Who's hungry?" Artimus asked rubbing his hands together.

"I am," Jeff said.

Baldwin shifted his eyes nervously. "Uhhhh, I'm not really that hungry."

Artimus pulled the spit off and started pushing roasted rodents onto metal plates. He handed plates to Nahima and Jeff. He took one for himself, and Dave took one.

There were a number of large boulders in the area of the fire-pit that Jeff assumed were their 'seats'. He plopped himself onto one and paused a moment to see what everybody else was doing.

Artimus and Dave were pulling limbs off and gnawing on them as if they were eating chicken legs. Jeff did the same and found it was delicious – the best breakfast he had eaten since arriving, much better than the bland fare he received at Artimus' place.

Everyone but Baldwin seemed to be thoroughly enjoying the meal. Nahima was a little tentative, but she seemed to be picking up speed as she got used to it.

Jeff leaned over to Baldwin and said in a quiet voice: "You should give it a try. It's pretty good."

"I think I can still see the dog's tooth marks in them," Baldwin said out of the side of his mouth.

Jeff wasn't sure if he was kidding but decided it would be best to not look too closely.

Jeff looked around the yard. He hadn't really gotten a clear look in the dark, but in the light, he saw that there was a large area about 400 feet in diameter that had been fenced off. Inside the perimeter, the ground was hard-packed dirt.

There was junk spread all around – rusted pieces of metal, plastic containers etcetera, mostly things that Jeff couldn't recognize. There was something that looked like a large, armored, military vehicle.

The armored vehicle had tank treads and was about the size of the trailer of an eighteen-wheeler. It was rectangular but with a nose that sloped to a point. A gun turret protruded from the top. Near that, Jeff saw Artimus' car. It was on some sort of flat-bed vehicle that looked almost like a boat with an upright control panel at the rear. The flat-bed vehicle was a little larger than Artimus' car, and Jeff inferred it flew since it didn't have any wheels.

The brune – Benji – was doing something outside the fence. It seemed that Benji wasn't a 'pet' but more of a 'friend' who had his own home somewhere.

"How'd you get so fat eating food like this?" Nahima

asked Dave.

"First off," Dave said as he shook a half-chewed leg at her, "this is some damn good food. And second, I'm all muscle."

He flexed his bicep, and Jeff had to admit it was impressive. His arms were bigger than Jeff's legs.

Then things got ugly.

Dave stood up, put his plate on a rock and lifted his shirt – exposing his enormous, pale belly.

"See," he said as he lifted his stomach and let it fall again. It wobbled like a bowl of refrigerated gravy. "Solid muscle, heh, heh, heh." He had the kind of laugh that would make mothers lock up their daughters... even the ugly ones... and any moderately attractive household pets.

Chapter 47:

"The pheerion fleet is coming in this way." Dave traced a line on a computer map that was built into a table. "General Blackbuck is moving into position here." He traced a line along the shore. "I figure we'll head there and see what we can do. Maybe seeing you will brighten his day a little." Dave looked at Artimus who responded with an expression Jeff couldn't read. "But I don't think the kids should go," Dave said.

"I'm going!" Baldwin said with a suddenness and *forcefulness* that took Jeff by surprise.

Nahima glared at Dave. "Well I know you're not talking about me, because I am NOT a 'kid'."

If everyone else was going, Jeff didn't see that he had a choice, and since Artimus thought he was 'The Raja', Jeff assumed he would be very disappointed if he didn't go. "I'm in," Jeff said with a coolness and bravery borne of not really having any damn options.

Jeff expected Artimus to make some symbolic protest, but he had a feeling Artimus wanted them all to go if they were willing.

Rather than directly protesting though, he said: "Tell them what you saw Dave... then let's see if everyone still wants to go."

"Well I was here." Dave pointed at a point on the shoreline. "At that point the pheerion fleet was still out here." He motioned to a general area in the ocean. "I saw air strikes approaching simultaneously from here and here." He traced two small arcs coming from opposite sides in at the spot where he had shown the fleet.

"They opened fire – roughly fifty aircraft all firing simultaneously. There was so much fire-power, it just looked like one big, glowing ball for a while... then they broke off the attack... not a single pheerion ship was damaged.

"They've got some kind of damn invincible force shield. About five minutes after that attack, the area lit up again. This time from Admiral Horn's fleet which had split and set up positions here and here.

"It was another intense bombardment, and again the whole area was glowing, but then, after about ten minutes of constant fire, Admiral Horn ceased fire to check for damage.

"Nothing! Still not a bit of damage, but then things turned. The pheerions started firing – using that gun they showed. It's for real. After about an hour, they had pretty much wiped out Admiral Horn's entire fleet."

Dave scanned the room. Artimus' expression was grim, while Baldwin and Nahima's were more shocked.

"We need to get to the small ship in front of the flagship," Jeff said, "that's where the key to the shield and gun are. We can deactivate them both from there."

All four heads snapped toward Jeff. Even Jeff seemed surprised at what had just come out of his mouth.

"How do you know that?" Dave asked with a raised eyebrow.

"I... don't know... I just... do."

Chapter 48:

Dave patted the side of his armored vehicle as he instructed Jeff and Baldwin regarding where to put the crates they were holding. "I named her Princess Trina – after a girl I used to know. Right Artimus?" He looked over his shoulder and raised his voice. "You know about Trina, right Artimus? Heh, heh, heh."

There was that laugh again.

It was the laugh of a guy who had just gotten back from the mall, taken the spy camera off his shoe, popped open a beer, turned on his computer and realized the girl in the light-blue skirt he had followed around for a half hour hadn't been wearing any underpants.

Dave was about the last person Jeff would want to see teaching first-grade, but there was something sort of reassuring about going to war with a guy who couldn't find his feminine side with both hands, a compass and a fifty-foot tall flashing neon sign with an arrow proclaiming: 'Here it is! Here's your feminine side!'

As they loaded the vehicle, Jeff noticed that Benji was pacing all around the vehicle without actually getting too close. Jeff could sense something was wrong and decided to try to communicate.

Jeff approached cautiously. While he had come to realize that Benji wasn't a threat, he still had a *frightening* physical presence.

"Benji," Jeff said, "is something wrong?"

Benji stopped his pacing and looked directly at Jeff. He made a few low, rumbling vocalizations: *'Go... I go... help.'*

Dave noticed Jeff's strange behavior. He dropped the box he had been carrying and watched with fascination.

"Do you understand," Jeff asked, "what we're doing?

193

We're going to war... fight."

Benji rumbled again. *'I go... I go help... help fight'*

As if to punctuate, he roared loudly and began swinging his arms violently.

That outburst got everyone's attention, and Jeff realized they were all watching.

"What are you doing?!?!" Dave ran toward them afraid Benji was about to maul Jeff.

Jeff turned calmly toward him. "He wants to go with us." He shrugged.

Dave looked at Benji then back at Jeff. "Look, I don't mind putting up with Artimus' delusions but..."

Jeff looked at Benji. "Dave doesn't think we understand each other. Do me a favor and put your hands up over your head to show him you understand."

Benji raised his hands over his head and shook them vigorously.

Jeff turned to look at Dave and gestured toward Benji.

Dave looked from Jeff to Benji and then back again. His mouth hung open stupidly. He looked at Benji who had dropped his hands and said: "Raise your hands up again."

Benji cocked his head but didn't raise his hands. He looked to Jeff.

"He wants you to raise your hands again to see if you can understand him." Jeff said.

At that, Benji raised his hands and waived them even more vigorously. As he did that, he let out an odd, howling... *laugh?*

Again, Dave looked back and forth between Jeff and Benji. "And he wants to go?" he asked Jeff.

Jeff nodded.

"And he understands what we're going to do?"

Jeff looked at Benji. "Do you understand we're going to fight... and it's going to be dangerous... and you might get hurt... or killed?"

Benji let out a loud roar that Jeff understood as an emphatic "Yes!"

Jeff turned to Dave and nodded.

Dave seemed to be thinking. Jeff could sense that he wasn't completely convinced, but he was thinking about it.

"Well," he said after several moments, "we could sure use the help. I guess he can come."

"He says you can come," Jeff said to Benji.

Benji let out a roar, ran toward Dave and gave his cringing friend a hug.

"I still don't think you're 'The Raja'," Dave said between gasping breaths.

But Jeff could tell he wasn't quite as sure of himself as he had been before.

Chapter 49:

They had been going for about six Earth hours, and it was uncomfortably quiet. Nobody seemed in the mood for conversation.

The armored vehicle – Princess Trina – wasn't built for comfort, and Jeff, Baldwin, Nahima and Benji rocked and bounced as it bumped and jostled along the dirt road.

Jeff looked around the space. The only two seats were up front where Artimus and Dave sat. There weren't any windows, but there were video screens scattered around that gave views of the outside. There were two, large, panel displays up front that gave the illusion of a large windshield.

The rest of the vehicle was little more than open space except for the gun turret with a seat that dangled from the ceiling and some canvas cots that had hinges so they could be folded up against the wall when not in use. There was a small table that could display maps and perform other computer tasks. Other than those items, the only contents were items they had loaded before leaving. There were a number of crates – mostly weapons and food – and the passengers who were sitting on crates or the floor.

They had also brought the flat-bed vehicle – Dave called it simply a 'lift-car' – on which Jeff had seen Artimus' car back at Dave's place. Dave gave Jeff a chance to drive the lift car and help steer it into Princess Trina, and Jeff loved the feeling of flying on that simple device. Now it was hanging from straps that were connected to the ceiling of the larger vehicle.

Jeff fidgeted nervously but tried to control his breathing and maintain as calm an appearance as possible. He imagined the others were doing the same and that was part of the reason for the uncomfortable silence – the other reason was that the road and engine noises were so loud, that it was difficult to talk and be understood. It wasn't worth the effort required for mindless small talk.

Jeff had often wondered what it would have felt like to be on one of the landing craft headed for Normandy on D-Day, and now he had at least something of an idea.

BUT, he told himself, *this isn't really that bad, because we're not heading to attack that sort of impenetrable defense... right?*

Actually he didn't have much of a sense for what they were heading into. It could be less deadly than D-Day... it could be *more*.

Every time he imagined that *'more deadly'* option, his stomach tightened, and his muscles would tense uncontrollably until he was able to force his mind to stop fixating on the unpleasant possibilities.

"You can do AMAZING things if you want to," Jeff's father had told him. "You just break the task down and only work on one part at a time. Don't get overwhelmed. Don't fixate on the things you don't know. Keep everything in perspective. Keep in mind, when you walk down the street, you aren't just walking down the street... if you consider yourself as the fixed point in space, you are actually turning the earth beneath you."

Jeff smiled as he thought about that. He was trying to follow his father's advice. He was trying to break the task down, not fixate on the things he didn't know and only work on one, small task.

At the moment his task was to not throw up.

Chapter 50:

"I think this is far enough to drive," Dave said. "Wouldn't want any sentries getting nervous and blowing us up... heh, heh, heh."

No, we wouldn't want that, Jeff thought.

The back door opened. It was hinged at the bottom and formed a ramp out of the vehicle.

Nahima led the way out, followed by Jeff, Baldwin and Benji, but it took a few more minutes for Artimus and Dave who were shutting things down.

They were on a deserted, wooded road, but Dave had already explained that they were very nearly to General Blackbuck's camp, and they should only be a short walk from the outermost check-point.

"Ummmm," Dave said looking at Benji, "I think you better stay here... at least until we can get past introductions."

Benji had a puzzled expression and looked at Jeff.

"He thinks you should stay here. We're meeting some soldiers, and they might be... frightened of you," Jeff explained.

Benji roared a protest and looked angrily at Dave, but Dave just stood there and looked him in the eye.

Benji roared even louder, and Jeff started to get nervous. *Maybe it wasn't such a good idea to bring him along.*

Benji looked like he was going to charge Dave. His fur was bristling. The last time Jeff had seen him like this, he was attacking the mantis. Jeff was glad to see it then, but now it was quite a frightening display.

After a couple lurches in Dave's direction – which failed to make Dave flinch – Benji calmed down, grumbled a couple times, and then sat down heavily on the ramp.

Dave patted him on the shoulder. "Sorry big guy."

"I'll stay here with him." Baldwin said and took a

seat on the ramp beside Benji.

"Would you?" Dave asked. "That would be great. I think that would make him feel better."

Artimus made an uncomfortable expression.

"Oh, stop worrying, Dad," Baldwin said. "I can take care of myself." He patted his gun.

Artimus eyed the surrounding trees. The sun was at the horizon, and it was just beginning to get dark. "If you see anything, just get in Princess Trina and close the door."

Jeff was impressed. While a gun, Benji, and the armored car would offer some protection, after seeing just some of the creatures that lived in the woods, Jeff felt safer with the group.

Then something happened to change his mind.

"Okay, let's leave our guns here," Dave said as he unbuckled his holster. "Don't want any sentries getting more nervous than necessary."

Jeff began reluctantly unbuckling his holster and looked over at Baldwin who was holding back a smile. *Bastard knew this would happen*, Jeff thought but couldn't really hold it against him. He knew he would have been tempted to do the same to avoid an unarmed stroll through the woods.

Then as he dropped the holster in the vehicle, he pulled his baseball bat out. "Any problem with me bringing this?" he asked.

"That should be okay," Dave said.

Nahima, Artimus, Dave and Jeff started down the road. As they walked, Dave pulled a meat-stick out of a pocket and a knife out of a sheath. He sliced off a chunk and popped it in his mouth. "Want some?" he asked as he chewed. He extended the stick toward Jeff.

Jeff was flattered. "Sure."

Dave sliced off a small disk and offered it to Jeff from the blade.

Jeff took the slice and popped it in his mouth.

It felt like someone had just dropped a hot coal in his

mouth. It was the spiciest thing he had ever tasted. He felt his face flush, and sweat starting to bead on his forehead.

"Hot enough for ya?" Dave grinned as he popped another slice into his mouth.

"It's goo..." Jeff broke into a coughing fit and couldn't finish his comment.

"Heh, heh, heh."

Chapter 51:

Jeff watched the lengthening shadows nervously.

He scanned the woods. He had heard several unusual noises along the way, and the hair was standing up on the back of his neck.

He felt like they were being watched.

"Are we almost there?" Jeff asked a bit shakily. His need to be reassured overwhelmed his desire to look calm and cool.

"Should be," Dave said.

Dave didn't seem certain enough for Jeff's comfort. Every noise, every shifting shadow grabbed Jeff's attention. His head snapped left, then right, up and down.

Dave noticed his nervousness and grinned. "Relax," he said, putting a hand on Jeff's shoulder. Then he leaned in and said – in a voice too quiet for anyone else to hear: "Anything around here comes after you... seeing it first won't do you any good."

He smiled ominously.

That hadn't done Jeff's nerves much good, and he went back to scanning the tree line – even more furiously than before. He felt his hands going numb from gripping his bat too tightly and made a conscious effort to loosen his grip.

Within a few minutes his grip had tightened again.

"HOLD!"

A loud, forceful voice startled Jeff.

Three soldiers stepped from behind some trees. "This is a restricted area." The one in the middle said. The soldiers had *very* large guns. They held them angled toward the ground, but that didn't make them any smaller.

"I'm Dave Kimble, and I'm with Artimus Winfred. We need to see General Blackbuck."

The two soldiers on the ends were stone faced. The

one in the center looked skeptical. "Is he expecting you?"

"No. But he'll want to see us. Trust me. You don't want to be the one who doesn't let us through."

The soldier continued to appear skeptical but seemed to think it would be better to turn the decision over to someone at a higher pay level. He spoke into a microphone on his shoulder. "This is Jenkins. I've got a Winfred and Kimble here who want to see the General."

"Understood. Checking now," a voice crackled from the other end.

"Nice weather, huh?" Dave said, looking at the sky.

The three soldiers were expressionless.

Jeff didn't know Artimus or Dave's exact status, but he found it a little strange that a general would take time to meet with them. He began to wonder if they were a little irrationally optimistic... or downright delusional.

Then he started to wonder what would happen if the General wasn't interested. He didn't want to end up in jail again.

After about five uncomfortable minutes, the voice crackled again.

"Transport on the way."

Chapter 52:

The transport vehicle reminded Jeff of the type of tram cars that shuttle amusement park visitors from large parking lots to ticket booths. It had hard seats molded into it, and it was open to the elements. But it was a single segment instead of a string of segments, and it had 4 pairs of large, off-road tires.

They bounced along the dirt road for about 3 miles, and then Jeff could see a huge encampment spread out in a large, open area. There were thousands of armed, uniformed soldiers. Some looked alert and ready – eying the transport as it passed – but others seemed to just be killing time – talking, playing games, eating, drinking.

The transport approached a dense grouping of tents. The driver stopped and spoke briefly with a sentry. The sentry motioned for Jeff and the others to follow him.

They walked wordlessly to a large tent. At the tent entrance, the sentry said simply: "Winfred, Kimble," to the armed guard at the entrance. The guard pulled the tent flap open and stepped aside.

The four walked through and saw three men in the room. Without being able to recognize the ranking insignia, Jeff immediately knew the one on the left was the general. His face and stance projected... *power*. His expression was stern and unsmiling, yet Jeff sensed a certain, latent... *kindness* in him.

"Artimus!" While the general didn't actually achieve a smile, his face did brighten noticeably.

"General," Artimus nodded soberly, but then was a little less able than the general to hold back his smile. "How are you?"

"Been better. What brings you out this way?"

"I was hoping we might be able to help," Artimus said.

"Well... based on what I've heard, I assume you didn't bring a Caesurmia army with you?"

"No... just us." Artimus seemed a bit embarrassed.

The general rested his hand on Artimus' shoulder. "I appreciate the gesture... really... I'm not just saying that. But unless you have a way to disable the pheerion's shield or guns..."

General Blackbuck turned and walked distractedly to a brightly lit table-top that had a glowing, electronic map projected onto it. The general moved his hand around on it absent-mindedly, and the image jostled and moved matching the movement of his finger.

"Well..." Artimus looked at Jeff but seemed reluctant to take the next step. "This boy... I believe he's ... The Raja."

Balls

General Blackbuck's head snapped around, and his eyes went from Artimus' to Jeff's. His eyes narrowed as he examined Jeff's face more closely.

Jeff could tell he didn't believe it for a minute.

"What..." the general began but stopped himself.

Jeff could tell he was about to ask Artimus what made him believe Jeff was The Raja, but he could also tell that he wanted to talk to Artimus about it alone.

"Would the rest of you please give me and my old friend a few moments alone?" the general asked.

Jeff, Dave, Nahima and the other two soldiers who had been with the General all left the tent. The two soldiers took up a position just outside the door, but Jeff, Dave and Nahima put a little more distance between themselves and the tent.

"He thinks Artimus is crazy," Jeff said after they had walked about twenty feet, "I can... sense it."

Dave laughed. "Well it don't take a psychic to figure that out. This whole 'The Raja' thing," he said as he rolled his eyes and waved his hands in a theatrical gesture, "Is getting old and annoying. Tell me – if you're so good at telling what people are thinking – what am I thinking about right now?"

Jeff thought for a moment.

"Nahima's back-end."

Dave's face fell abruptly. "Well it don't take a psychic to figure that out either."

Chapter 53:

"Well, I got a little bit... not a lot, but a little bit," Artimus announced to the others when he had finished his meeting. "Let's head back to Princess Trina and I'll fill you in."

The four loaded onto the transport which headed back toward the armored vehicle.

When they arrived, Artimus thanked the transport driver and sent him back.

"Let's get inside, and I can tell you what's going on," Artimus said.

Once inside, Artimus had them crowd around the map table.

"Here's the situation. Blackbuck says the pheerion fleet is anchored here." He pointed to a spot on the map. "Blackbuck has troops and armament stationed all through here." Artimus indicated a broad arc that was positioned to fend off any landing by the pheerion troops.

"General Rasp is leading the pheerions. He's the one we saw demonstrating the gun on that video message. Rasp has been sending out very small scouting groups. Blackbuck suspects that Rasp is trying to determine troop positioning – not for a landing attack but so that he can tear them apart with the cannon. Blackbuck is very concerned about that cannon. He feels that he can easily out-match the pheerions, but not with the shield and cannon in place.

"Blackbuck's missiles, shells and energy weapons aren't getting through the shield at all. He feels completely helpless. He is sending his own scouting troops down to meet Rasp's scouts, and he says he's having good success with that. But he feels he's just delaying the inevitable.

"This," Artimus said as he held up an electronic box, "will help link us with Blackbuck's troops. This shows us their locations." There were red dots scattered on a map. Artimus used some buttons on the side to zoom in, and the dots became sharper and more scattered. Then he zoomed out, and the dots blended together into less clearly defined red patterns.

"This green dot is us," Artimus pointed to a dot on the screen. "As long we have this box, we'll show up as friendlies on other troop's screens, so... hopefully... they won't be shooting at us.

"Now I need to scan all of your retinas into this. If I get killed, you'll need to be able to use it. The screen turns off every 15 seconds, and if you want to view it, you need to scan your retina and type in code '3281'. It will also periodically vibrate to indicate you need to verify yourself." Artimus scanned their retinas as he was speaking. "With proper verification, we can use this device to request support. I'll make sure you all understand the details when we have a few spare moments.

"So... that's where we are. If, by tomorrow, the shield and gun are both still active, it's likely General Blackbuck's troops will be wiped out. Jeff thinks the gun and shield are located on the small ship in front of the flag-ship. As far as we know, the shield is impenetrable, and the gun is more powerful than anything we've ever seen before.... any ideas?"

Artimus scanned the assembled faces, lingering on Jeff's each time he would catch his eyes.

There was an awkward silence.

For several minutes nobody said anything. They just looked at the map, the floor. *What possible options could there be?*

"I think I know..." Jeff said but then paused.

All eyes focused on him.

"Know what?" Artimus' previously sullen face brightened.

Jeff shook his head. "I don't know... it's like... it's like I know the answer, but I can't think of it. It's like when you know someone's name, but you just can't think of it."

Artimus' face sank again. "Well, see if you can figure it out." He scanned the other faces to see if anyone else had anything, but again the awkward silence filled the vehicle.

"Under..." Jeff said tentatively.

"Under?" Artimus' face brightened again. "What does that mean?"

"I think we can get under the shield..." He suddenly got more excited. It seemed to be coming very clearly to him. "Can we get a submarine?"

The others looked at him puzzled.

"Submarine?" Dave asked.

"Submarine... a... a... boat that goes under the water."

Baldwin laughed, but Artimus shot him a stern look.

"There are research vessels that go under the water to observe sea-life... but they're typically tethered to a ship and can only go where the ship goes. We'd have to find a ship, get it to where we need it to be, and use it without getting spotted." Artimus shook his head. "I'm afraid we just don't have enough time to put something like that together."

"Well if the shield doesn't go below the water, we could get up to the edge, and swim under." Baldwin suggested.

Jeff didn't like that idea. He was a decent swimmer, but swimming under a force shield and then attacking a ship... from the water... in the middle of the night. That didn't sound like his idea of a fun way to pass an evening.

"I like it," Nahima said. "How could the shield extend under the water? I'll bet it just comes down to the water's edge. The lift-car should be able to take us right up to the edge, and then a couple of us can swim under and try to get to the ship." She looked around at the others.

Everyone seemed to think it was at least *something*. Though, like Jeff, no-one seemed overly enthusiastic about the idea.

"Well," Nahima said, "maybe we should check it out. We could head to the water's edge, get a good look at the fleet and see if it seems possible, and then go from there."

"I think that sounds like a good idea," Artimus said.

"I agree, at least we'd be doing something," Dave added.

Baldwin and Jeff looked nervously at each other.

Chapter 54:

Princess Trina eased toward the water's edge. Nahima, Baldwin and Jeff were crowded behind Artimus and Dave. They could make out the vague outline of the pheerion fleet on the front screens. Artimus' troop locator indicated they were far from any troops.

"Well," Artimus said, "should we go get a better look?"

Dave swung Princess Trina around so that the rear door faced the fleet.

They readied their guns and cautiously exited the vehicle. Dave set up a viewing device on a tripod and focused in on the fleet.

Dave tapped the screen. "Is this our boat?"

Jeff looked at Dave, then at the screen. "Yeah... yeah, I think that's it. So you believe me now?"

Dave rolled his eyes. "No. I still think you're full of plooch, but what do I have better to do? Heh, heh, heh."

The others crowded around the screen to get a good look and alternated between looking at the screen and looking out across the water.

Jeff thought it looked... SO far away. *Am I going to have to go?* he wondered. *Probably... after all it's my idea. Do I have any idea what I'm actually talking about? In some ways, it feels... right... but am I just kidding myself? Have any of my feelings really meant anything?*

Jeff realized that, while he had many 'feelings', none of them had really been proven correct beyond any general common sense. *But I can communicate with Benji... right? Or am I just imagining that too?*

He began to doubt himself, and he began to shake nervously. *Am I just leading all these people on?*

He started to wonder if he should just quit. Just admit he had no idea what he was talking about and end it there. *What would happen then?*

Jeff heard a strange noise in the distance...

Then all hell broke loose.

It was so quick, that it was mostly a blur to Jeff, but he heard several shots coming from his right, and there were 'pinging' sounds coming from the vehicle as ammunition hit it.

We're under attack!

"GET DOWN!" Artimus shouted as he and Dave drew their weapons and began returning fire.

Jeff dove for the ground and got a mouthful of dirt.

The flashes of light illuminated a number of pheerions at the tree-line. When Jeff saw them, his heart started beating furiously. He fumbled for his own gun, but his hands didn't feel like they were working.

Benji roared furiously and charged toward the pheerions. Artimus and Dave jumped up and ran after him. Jeff wasn't sure if they had intended to do that before Benji charged... *or are they just reacting to him?*

Dave and Artimus fired furiously as they ran. Jeff saw a couple pheerions fall, a couple others fired off shots while many others seemed to be fumbling with their guns but not firing. There were at least twenty of them.

Do they only have single shots? Jeff wondered. Unlike Artimus' guns, the pheerions guns were loud and sounded much more like the guns Jeff knew from home. *Gunpowder? Muskets?*

"Come on!" Nahima jumped up and started toward the action. Baldwin jumped up to join her.

But Jeff was frozen. He wanted to jump up and join the others but his body simply wouldn't.

Pop, pop, pop. The pheerion guns were loud but far enough away from Jeff that their reports were dulled and muted.

"Are you coming?" Nahima shouted over her shoulder with a puzzled expression as she gestured for Jeff to follow. Then she turned back to the action and ran to catch up with Baldwin who was getting ahead of her.

Jeff wanted to go with them. Jeff felt like he *had* to go with them, but his legs and arms wouldn't obey his command that they move. With great mental effort, he *willed* his arms and legs to push him off the ground, and... *slowly*... with great effort, he began to move forward using all the mental energy he could muster.

Eventually he was able to make some forward progress, and once he had broken through the barrier, he was able to continue moving, somewhat normally. He drew his gun and tried to catch up with Nahima and Baldwin who were closing the distance between them and the others.

Jeff could see the pheerions scattering. Some were running, some were falling. A few stood their ground and fired. Jeff saw Benji lurch a few times, and Jeff had the sick feeling that he had been hit fairly badly.

There was a pheerion to Jeff's right who was a good distance from the main group but frighteningly close to Jeff. The pheerion raised his gun and took aim at Jeff.

What did Artimus say when he was showing me the gun? Setting 3 will stun a pheerion, and setting 8 should be enough to kill one but use 10 ... just to make sure.

Jeff fumbled nervously with his gun as he ran and dialed his to "4". Artimus wouldn't have approved, but he was too busy, at the moment, to yell at Jeff.

Jeff raised his gun and aimed at the pheerion. He flinched as the pheerion fired, but Jeff didn't feel any bullets cutting into him. He realigned his shot as the pheerion fumbled with his gun – apparently reloading. Jeff fired once.

Missed!

He fired again, and that time the pheerion dropped.

Ahead of Jeff and to his left, Benji had reached the tree-line and was swinging furiously at the pheerions who remained. Bodies flew into the air as Benji flailed.

By the time Jeff made it to the tree-line himself, there

were no pheerions remaining standing. He saw a pheerion body and shuddered. He wasn't sure if it was dead or just unconscious, but either way, it was still frightening. Jeff had the nervous feeling its eyes were about to snap open, and it was going to attack him.

Probably watching too many bad movies.

Silence.

It was an eerie, uncomfortable silence.

Let's get back in the vehicle. Jeff felt like saying but held his tongue.

Dave and Artimus scanned the woods, their weapons raised. "Okay," Artimus said. "Keep your eyes open, and let's do a slow, calm pull-back to Princess Trina."

Dave grabbed Benji's hand and pulled him toward the vehicle. Jeff could see several spots of matted blood on Benji's fur.

Artimus stood by the tree-line until everybody else had started moving. When he started moving himself, Jeff could see that he was limping, and there were at least two bloody spots on his pants.

Chapter 55:

"Let's get away from the shore and re-group," Artimus said as he closed the door behind him.

Dave was already firing up the engines.

"Benji's hurt," Jeff said as soon as he got the chance. He had to brace himself to prevent falling over as Dave pulled back on the accelerator.

Artimus nodded. He was pulling a medical kit off the wall.

"How are you?" Jeff asked, eying the blood-stains on Artimus' pants.

"I'm okay. EVERYBODY ELSE OK?" he asked as he quickly shaved a spot on Benji's leg with an electric razor and reached for a hypodermic.

Benji was groaning, and he lurched and growled angrily as he felt the needle.

"Can you try to let him know what I'm doing?" Artimus asked.

Jeff kneeled by Benji and put an arm gently on Benji's elbow. "Just try to relax. It might hurt for a minute, but it will help to make you better." Benji rumbled, and Jeff knew that he understood.

Jeff cringed when he saw what Artimus was doing. He had cut Benji's leg and was fishing for a bullet in one of his wounds with forceps. He reached for a hand-held scanner and waved it over the wound. A glowing dot appeared on the screen which Jeff assumed was the bullet. Artimus waved it around until he had a good fix on the location, and then went in again with the forceps.

This time he was successful. He extracted the bullet and dropped it. It landed with a "clunk", and then began to roll around the floor of the bouncing vehicle.

Artimus peeled open a patch and finished off the wound before looking for the next one. "Okay," he said as he worked, "let's think about this. I think we should head to a quiet area, launch the lift-car and head for the fleet.

"I'd say a very small party, two or three should try to swim under the shield and try to get to the shield ship, disable the shield, and/or gun, and then get back to the lift car."

"Yeah, that sounds easy," Baldwin said sarcastically.

Artimus shot him a look.

"I know it's not going to be easy. It may not even be possible, but we have to *try*. I'm volunteering to be one to go on-board."

"You're injured!" Nahima protested. "And besides, you should stay here with Benji. I'll go."

Artimus opened his mouth to speak but held himself. He didn't like what she was saying, but he couldn't argue.

"You can't swim," Baldwin said to Nahima. "I'm a ten times better swimmer than you. I'll do it."

Jeff's heart was pounding. He knew he *should* go, but he sure as hell didn't *want* to go. He opened his mouth to speak but paused... then tried again... "I'll go... I sort of think I should."

Artimus nodded and took his eyes off of Benji for a moment to look at Jeff, then went back to his work.

"Oh, hell," Dave said from the driver's seat. "I think you're all crazy and this is a suicide mission, but I can't sit here and let the kids do everything. I'll go."

Artimus looked around at the four of them. "Okay, how about this. Nahima, you're a good pilot, and Baldwin's right, you *can't* swim. Why don't you pilot the lift-car and Baldwin, Jeff and Dave will go onboard. I'll stay here with Benji and man the cannon." He glanced up at the turret. "I'll be prepared to call in troops if we need them."

Everyone nodded agreement.

"We won't be able to take guns," Dave said from up front.

Jeff looked up and saw Dave's grinning face peering back at them over his shoulder.

"The guns would be shorted out as soon as they hit the water. We'll have to leave them on the lift-car.

"Heh, heh, heh."

Chapter 56:

The lift-car floated, silent and low, over the water.

Jeff was shivering.

It wasn't from the cold, it was from an intense nervousness, but he figured he could blame it on the cold if anyone noticed. *All this technology and they haven't figured out how to make a submergible gun?*

Nahima slowed the vehicle as they approached the clearly visible, though somewhat transparent, force-shield. She pulled to within a few feet of the shield and held the position.

Dave pulled a large pole off the floor of the lift-car and dropped it into the water. He twisted it and pushed it through the area where the force shield would be if the shield penetrated under the water. It moved easily through, and Dave's face broke out in a big, goofy grin.

"Weee zola! Looks like we're good. Better leave our guns here." Dave unbuckled his gun-belt and dropped it on the floor.

Baldwin followed his lead, and Jeff was about to drop his but stopped. He pulled the gun out and placed it gently on the floor. Then he patted the baseball bat that was hanging from his belt.

"You're gonna swim with that extra weight?" Dave asked with arched eyebrows.

Jeff considered the idea of swimming with the extra weight vs. being on a boat full of pheerions completely unarmed. He pulled the bat out bounced it in his hands, evaluating both the weight and solidness.

"Yep."

Dave rolled his eyes in disgust, and then *snatched* the bat out of Jeff's hands. "Raja my back-end," he mumbled under his breath.

Then, to Jeff's surprise, rather than tossing it on the

deck or, worse, into the ocean, he tucked the bat into his belt and tugged on it to make sure it was secure.

Nahima scanned the decks nervously looking for any signs of pheerion movement.

"They're drunk," Jeff said.

The others looked at him.

"I can just sort of... sense it. Most of the crew members are drunk."

Everyone had gotten used to those sort of odd pronouncements, and even Jeff was used to hearing things come out of his mouth that he hadn't expected.

He still wasn't sure how much he could trust the strange feelings, but he hoped that one was right. Maybe they'd have a chance if the crews were drunk.

"Okay," Dave said, "we're just going to get in the water, pop under and come right back up on the other side. Then we can all swim together to that boat, right over there." He pointed.

Jeff got a sudden feeling that Dave wasn't real confident in his own swimming skills, and it made him feel a little better to know that even Dave might actually be sort of nervous.

Of course that made no *logical* sense, but Jeff was taking any comfort he could find.

"We should be able to climb the anchor ropes," Dave said. "Nahima, you get good and clear. When we're ready, I'll turn on the beacon." He held up a small ball that had a radio signal and light for sea rescues. "I'm going to just use the radio beacon so the pheerions can't aim at the light. If you get close, I may turn on the light... if it looks like we're clear.

"Everybody ready?"

No, Jeff thought as he hopped into the water.

Chapter 57:

Wooo, hooo, hooo, hoooo...

The water was *frigid*.

As soon as Jeff hit it, he could feel the air being sucked out of his lungs.

Considering he still needed to duck under the shield, swim a couple hundred yards, climb up an anchor rope – all without being seen by any guards – then somehow find and disable a shield and gun that were beyond the comprehension of a technologically advanced society.

It wasn't a good time to be out of breath.

He forced his lungs to suck in air and tried to get his breathing into a comfortable range. It became easier as his body acclimated to the water..

For a moment, Jeff felt hopeless desperation.

Suck it up, he told himself. *Push through it. There are countless people depending on this. Your body can handle it. Only your mind is holding you back.*

The salt-water stung Jeff's wounds, but they were amazingly well healed considering the short time it had been since he suffered them.

He took a deep breath and went under. He swam until he was sure he was well beyond the edge of the shield and then surfaced. He saw Nahima on the other side of the shield backing carefully away, but he couldn't see either Dave or Baldwin. He got panicky for a second, but then he saw Dave's head surface about twenty feet away, and Baldwin came up ten feet from Dave.

Baldwin led the way and Dave and Jeff followed, using gentle, easy strokes to keep the splashing sounds to a minimum.

By the time they were halfway there, Jeff was gasping for air. His limbs were beginning to get numb and sloppy, but he pushed on.

Baldwin reached the anchor rope and held on until

the others arrived. Dave made it shortly after him, but it was getting harder and harder for Jeff. He was going much slower than when he had started.

Dave gestured and held out an arm, but Jeff was still far out of reach. After another fifteen seconds he was there but with very little energy left.

"Baldwin, you go ahead and start up, then Jeff, then I'll bring up the rear," Dave whispered. "Be careful and be QUIET when you get to the deck. If any guards are nearby, give us this signal:" Dave made a 'stop' motion. "If it's clear, give us this:" Dave made a 'forward' motion.

Baldwin started up, and then Jeff latched on. His arms and legs felt like rubber, and he feared he wouldn't be able to make it.

He pushed on and, bit by bit, edged his way up the rope.

Baldwin was at the top and not moving. Jeff was forced to just hang on below him, but was afraid he might not be able to hold on much longer. He nearly shouted at Baldwin to just go already, but he resisted the urge, took a deep breath, re-adjusted his grip and focused on just hanging on. He tried not to think about the burning pain in his arms and hands.

After what seemed like an eternity, Baldwin made the 'forward' gesture and slipped over the edge of the deck.

Jeff and Dave lifted themselves over the edge and dropped silently.

The three of them crouched for a moment, taking their bearings. Dave handed Jeff his bat and then his head snapped around as he heard a noise.

A pheerion was approaching from the right side.

Dave grabbed Jeff's arm and pushed Baldwin from behind to nudge them, gently but purposefully, to an area behind some barrels. They tucked in behind the barrels and held their breath as the footfalls approached. The pheerion paused and looked over the stern of the boat.

He suspects something! Jeff thought as he gripped the

handle of his bat.

Then he realized the pheerion was just taking in the view.

A loud, hissing voice from Jeff's right nearly made him gasp.

He understood what the voice was saying. *'Did you have enough to drink?'* the new arrival said to the first as he slapped him on the shoulder.

'Idiot, I'm on guard duty,' the other hissed in response.

'You call me an idiot? What are you guarding? Nothing can get through the shield.'

The guard hissed back. That time, Jeff didn't hear any words in his head but just sensed anger.

The other pheerion took the hint and left the other alone again. Jeff was pretty sure he was staggering, though he wasn't quite sure how they normally walked.

The other pheerion stood at the stern for another minute or two and then moved on.

"Okay, now what?" Dave asked.

Jeff had absolutely no idea.

Chapter 58:

Jeff cautiously emerged from behind the barrel to get a feel for what they were dealing with. *The decks seem deserted... good. Now where is the shield generator and gun?*

Jeff looked for any tell-tale signs, but nothing seemed obvious. The boat was similar to wooden boats of the eighteenth and nineteenth centuries. There was a small "tower" in the center – three levels high.

If I had a big gun, Jeff thought, *I'd have it up as high as possible.*

He leaned out to try to get a better look. *Is that it?* He hoped that he would get one of his feelings – something that would give him more confidence than just wandering blindly, and taking the very real risk that they'd be discovered. *Every step we take... every second we spend on here increases our chances of being found.*

Jeff closed his eyes and concentrated, hoping for some divine inspiration.

Nothing.

"Damn!" he said out loud but in a whisper.

"What's wrong!" Dave and Baldwin both said simultaneously and clearly alarmed.

Jeff looked at them. "Oh... nothing... nothing."

There was no reason to have them all know how uncertain he was, he decided.

Jeff pointed to the top floor of the raised section. "I think it's up there."

"Let's trundle." Dave pulled a large knife from a sheath. "Why don't you let me lead?"

Jeff wasn't about to argue.

Chapter 59:

The three of them had their backs pasted to the wall, as they edged their way around the center structure. The stairs to each level were located at one corner. There was a narrow cat-walk and no way to go from the top of the first set of stairs to the bottom of the second set without going completely around the tower at the second level.

Pretty dumb design, Jeff thought to himself.

They were within about ten feet of the stairs when a door opened and a pheerion emerged.

Before Jeff, Baldwin or the pheerion knew what was happening, Dave had grabbed him from behind and cut his throat.

Dave and Baldwin both froze and watched Dave with looks of shocked horror.

Dave looked around considering what he should do with the body, and – realizing that a body lying around the deck would be a sure sign to anyone else who happened by that something was wrong – he dragged it to the edge and heaved it over. He returned, looked at the blood, but there wasn't much he could do about it.

"Ready?" Dave ignored their shock and didn't wait for an answer but rather charged ahead and quickly got up the first flight of steps.

I guess it was a rhetorical question, Jeff thought to himself. He moved briskly but quietly to catch up with Dave and Baldwin who had managed to stay closer to Dave.

They climbed the first set of steps quickly but then slowed as they came to the middle landing. They began creeping around the structure, alert for any noises or movements. There didn't seem to be any lights on that second level, but Jeff could see a light on the third level above them.

Jeff looked up. He sensed there was at least one,

maybe more, pheerions close by, and he sensed at least one mind that was much sharper and more alert than the ones they had encountered so far.

Dave led, Baldwin was behind him, and Jeff brought up the rear. There was an open door ten feet from the top of the steps, and there was light coming from it, but Jeff couldn't hear any sounds. Dave climbed the steps – much more slowly and methodically than he had climbed the first set.

He made it to the landing and began edging his way along the wall. As he got close to the door, he tried to get a look without actually being exposed himself. Then, without a word and leaving Jeff and Baldwin wondering what he was doing, he *charged* into the room. Baldwin ran after him, and Jeff tried to catch up but tripped and fell on the last step.

Jeff saw a flash of light, then made it to his feet and ran to the doorway just in time to see another flash and an energy blast hitting Baldwin square in the chest.

Baldwin went limp and fell.

Jeff could see Dave... *unconscious?... dead?...* slumped on the floor five feet from Baldwin.

Jeff looked up to see the source of the blasts and...

He was face to face with the pheerion of his nightmares – General Rasp.

But he was different.

His eyes were different. Not as cold. Not as evil.

Scared?

Could that be?

As Jeff looked into those red eyes that had given him so many sleepless nights, he had the strongest feeling that the... creature... was frightened... of him for some reason.

The two of them looked at each other, and to Jeff's displeasure, he felt the creature's fear begin to fade.

Is it my fear I'm sensing? Jeff wondered.... or... *maybe... he was afraid of Dave but realized Dave wasn't a threat anymore.*

Jeff slowly reached for his bat and eased it out of his

belt. He felt the fear swelling again.

The creature spoke in the wheezing croaking voice that Jeff had come to know so well: *'What are you doing here?'*

Jeff had a very strange, very strong feeling that the creature... *recognized* him.

Is it possible he's been dreaming about me, also, Jeff wondered.

"I'm here to stop you."

Jeff felt the fear surge again... fear mixed with... surprise?

Yes, surprise because he could understand Jeff.

'You can't stop me boy...'

It was right out of Jeff's dream, though not quite as intense. General Rasp wasn't nearly as sure of himself as he had seemed in the dream.

'Not while I have the power of the artifact.'

General Rasp raised his hand.

He has it!

He has my father's locket!

That's how he recognized me. He recognized me from the photo.

Once again, they faced each other silently.

Then Rasp struck.

A beam of energy shot from the locket, and Jeff raised the bat instinctively.

And it stopped the beam!

The two of them looked at the beam which was going from the locket to the bat.

The fear came in smashing waves.

Jeff had no idea what to do now. The pheerion was clearly frightened, but Jeff didn't know why. Jeff didn't have the confidence that should have been the flip-side of that fear.

The energy beam continued to hang there. It shifted and crackled but stayed linked to Jeff's bat which he gripped with both hands.

Jeff wished he knew why the pheerion was afraid... because Jeff wanted to do whatever it was that was so frightening to him.

There was a pushing force being transmitted into the baseball bat from the beam which continued to crackle and waver. Jeff's arms were beginning to tire.

He pushed the bat in the direction of the General Rasp, and when he did that, the energy beam shot back at the creature.

There was a bright flash, and the general was knocked back, but at the same moment, Jeff's action seemed to cause a concussion wave that also blew back and knocked Jeff down.

Everything went black.

Chapter 60:

Jeff was drifting in and out of consciousness.

As he began to gain some clarity, he saw Baldwin moving. He tried to speak but couldn't.

Baldwin was over him, shaking him.

"Are you alright?"

The locket, Jeff thought, but the words didn't come out.

He tried to point, tried to tell Jeff to get the locket. He had a strong... very strong, very clear feeling that the locket was the key – not only to General Rasp's energy blasts but also to the shield and gun.

We have to get that locket!

Rasp was beginning to stir, but Baldwin was too concerned with Jeff to notice.

"Get... the... locket..." Jeff finally managed to force the words out, and he was able to point feebly in the direction of the, now clearly conscious, pheerion.

Baldwin looked over his shoulder and appeared to see the locket in the pheerion's hand, but was, himself, paralyzed – not from the earlier blast but from fear.

Baldwin pushed himself up, but his knees buckled as he made his way toward Rasp.

The pheerion's legs and arms started to twitch as he regained control.

Baldwin approached, slowly, tentatively.

Hurry up! Jeff's mind was shouting, but his voice was silent.

Baldwin was breathing quickly and mentally forcing each footstep to push a little ahead of the previous one. It was like learning to walk all over again. What normally came naturally now seemed to be a conscious process.

He was close to the pheerion, but the closer he got, the slower he moved.

Jeff tried to *will* him closer – like a golfer or bowler trying to get his ball to move in the right direction while it was already on the way.

Rasp's eyes were open and looking at Baldwin. His limbs twitched, but he clearly didn't have full control of them... yet.

Baldwin leaned down...

And snatched the locket with a quick, sweeping motion.

He ran back to Jeff's side, keeping one eye over his shoulder on the pheerion.

Jeff forced himself up into a sitting position and took the locket Baldwin offered him.

He opened it and saw his own, younger, face looking back.

Chapter 61:

Dave was beginning to stir.

"See if Dave's okay," Jeff instructed Baldwin. "We've got to get out of here... now."

Jeff wanted to keep an eye on Rasp. He was sure that the locket was the key to his energy beams, but he didn't know if he had any other weapons or abilities. The cannon was in the corner of the room, as were some bulky electronic devices. Jeff could see a sliding door above the gun that opened to allow the barrel to protrude.

Jeff was sure that everything was linked, in some way, to the locket. If he could get it off the ship, the shield and cannon would be disabled.

'Do it,' the pheerion croaked.

"Do what?" Jeff asked, puzzled.

'Kill me.'

"I... I don't want to kill you, I just wanted to stop you from using... that gun."

The pheerion looked away, and Jeff sensed anger... shame.

'You've already done it. Now it's just a matter of whose hand finishes it, yours or the king's... KILL ME!'

Baldwin was helping Dave to his feet.

"Let's get out of here." Jeff said urgently.

The three of them headed for the door, but before they could get there, two gun wielding pheerions blocked their path.

Chapter 62:

'*Excellent, excellent.*' Rasp hissed.

The three humans backed away from the new arrivals back into the room toward Rasp.

Rasp was on his feet and approaching Jeff.

Jeff concentrated. He tried to channel the energy from the locket and shoot energy beams as Rasp had, but nothing happened.

Rasp took the locket from Jeff and then spoke to the guards.

'*Very good work. Do you know what would have happened if they had gotten this off the ship?*' He held up the locket.

The guards stared dumbly.

'*If they had gotten this off the ship, our shield would have dropped, and we would have been defenseless. If we hadn't turned around at that moment and gotten out of these waters, the human's weapons could have destroyed us. We would have had to try to escape before they realized what happened and took advantage of our weakness.*'

Jeff found the statement...very strange. *Why is he telling them that right now with such emphasis on what might have happened? Isn't he embarr...*

Before Jeff could finish the thought, the room was filled with a brilliant flash.

And the two guards slumped.

Chapter 63:

Jeff was confused. He looked back at Rasp.

Rasp approached, knelt, bowed his head and held the locket up to Jeff. *'This belongs to you.'*

Jeff took it from him, speechless, as Baldwin and Dave gawked.

'Take me with you... please.' He looked up at Jeff.

Jeff had the feeling that 'please' was a word that wasn't often used in the pheerion language.

"He wants to go *with us.*" Jeff explained to Baldwin and Dave as they stared.

"He... we..." Dave couldn't seem to find the words.

"We should be able to trust him," Jeff reasoned. "Look at what he just did for us."

"Let's do whatever will get us the hell out of here quickest. Bring him along." Dave said with clear exasperation and ran out the door.

The four of them were running so fast they were almost floating with their feet just skimming the ground with each step. The noise had brought several pheerions out to see what was going on, but Dave just charged ahead, making sure Jeff and Baldwin were with him. Rasp brought up the rear.

The pheerions seemed too confused to act, and Dave had made it to the railing with little difficulty. He helped Jeff and Baldwin over the railing and then followed them. He paid little attention to Rasp who followed right behind him.

Jeff hit the water and sank much farther than he would have liked. He tried to remain calm in the cold, eerie quiet of the ocean and then worked his way back to the surface.

He broke through the surface in time to hear Dave shouting: "We've got to get clear of the ships!" Dave reached into his pocket. "I've just activated the beacon."

Jeff heard some shots coming from the ship, but he couldn't see any bullets hitting the water or his friends. He hoped that a little more distance would make them difficult to see in the dark and put them out of range of the guns.

Baldwin was well ahead of the others with Dave relatively close behind, and Jeff was watching the distance between himself and Dave lengthen. He was running out of strength, and he began to think he wouldn't make it.

Then he felt something on his arm. Rasp had taken hold of his upper arm and was pulling him along. Rasp was an excellent swimmer.

They approached Dave, and Rasp reached out with his free hand. Dave's arm flinched instinctively when he felt Rasp's touch. Dave was confused at first, but he wasn't too proud to accept assistance considering the circumstances. Soon the three of them had caught up with Baldwin at a point near where the shield – which was no longer there – would have been.

The four of them treaded water.

There was no sign of Nahima.

Chapter 64:

Dave looked nervously up at the ship closest to them. "I'm thinking we should put a little more distance between us and the ships."

While it made sense, Jeff didn't really like the idea of getting farther out into open water. The four of them continued to move – but at a slower pace.

"Where is she?" Jeff asked. He turned his head from side to side looking for some sign of Nahima.

"She'll be here," Dave said.

"Unless something happened to her," Baldwin added.

Jeff didn't want to think about it. After all they'd been through, it was just overwhelming to think they might have made it this far just to drown or be re-captured.

An eerie silence hung over the black water.

"I wonder if the beacon's working," Dave commented. He shook it and looked at it, but Jeff suspected Dave didn't have a clue if it was actually working.

More silence.

Jeff began to wonder if they had sharks in their oceans... *or maybe something worse.*

Silence.

Then Jeff thought he saw something.

No. Just a reflection. There was a feeling of desperate terrifying isolation out there in the ocean. In some ways, it didn't seem as frightening as fighting some sort of monster, but would a slow drowning death leave him any less dead than a fearsome struggle against a warrior creature?

Jeff was getting tired... *very tired.* His limbs were numb, and they began to refuse to do what he wanted of them. He was concentrating on each movement, and the harder he concentrated, the more difficult it became.

Silence.

Then he saw it.

Coming in low and fast.

Nahima!

She hovered and helped Baldwin, then Jeff, then Dave onto the deck of her vehicle... then she jumped back.

She had just seen Rasp.

Jeff had never seen her scream, but he thought she was real close at that moment. He smiled to himself.

"It's okay. He's with us."

Chapter 65:

"Fantastic! Just fantastic!" Artimus beamed as they told him the story. "I'm going to contact Blackbuck, and he'll wipe out the fleet."

"No!" Jeff said suddenly. "We have to give them time to get away." He looked at Rasp.

Artimus looked from Jeff to Rasp and understood.

But he was a soldier at heart, and the idea of allowing an enemy to flee to fight another day bothered him.

He fidgeted uncomfortably. "If you feel strongly about it. I'll watch to see when they pull up anchor."

"I think they'll be moving soon," Jeff said, "the General made it clear to them that they'd be defenseless if the locket was taken."

Artimus went up to the front to check the monitors, and Jeff gestured to Rasp.

The two of them found a private corner to talk, and Jeff pulled the locket out of his pocket.

"Where did you get this?" He asked.

'From my king... I don't know where he got it...and now... I'm afraid there will be a price on my head so high I won't be able to show my face in public... so it won't be easy to ask him.'

Jeff thought about that for a while. At least he knew something now. He had a little bit to work with. "How does it work? How do you make it shoot those... beams?"

'You need this.' He showed Jeff an electronic device on his glove. *'And you need a machine that is back on the ship. The King didn't want anyone to have too much power, so he built safeguards into it. He controls the devices and has ways to disable them.'*

"So it's useless now?" Jeff asked.

'Useless?' Rasp seemed confused. *'It may no longer have powers, but is it not still the Artifact?'*

Chapter 66:

The food wasn't the best Jeff had ever had, but the celebratory dinner in the mess tent was, almost without question, the greatest moment of Jeff's life.

Jeff couldn't stop grinning as people pounded him on the back, congratulated and thanked him.

Artimus, Dave, Baldwin and Nahima were all getting similar treatment. Rasp had stayed in Princess Trina with Benji. Artimus thought that would be for the best.

No matter what happens from now on, Jeff thought, *I've got this moment. Today... I... we made a difference. Nobody will ever be able to take that away.*

"I guess there's no question now," Artimus said to Jeff. He had to shout to be heard above the cacophony. "You can't deny you're The Raja. Remember Prophecy 11: 'Only The Raja has the power to wrest the Numino from the Warlord'."

Jeff thought about that for a moment. *Well, actually, Baldwin's the one who took the locket from Rasp,* he thought to himself.

He looked at Baldwin who was looking back at him. He could tell Baldwin was thinking the same thing, but Baldwin was also thinking something else: *'Don't you dare tell him about that.'*

Jeff took another bite of food.

Of course I'm still the one who fell from the sky... unless you count when we ran out of energy on our way to Dave's...

Jeff looked at Baldwin who looked back at him with a 'What's that look about?' expression.

Jeff had some more food – a hearty mouthful this time. It was starting to taste a little better.

He was getting used to it.

He reached into a leather pocket on his belt and pulled out the locket.

He opened it and looked at the young... *so very young...* face.

My father must be here... somewhere.

Dedicated with sincere appreciation for the
encouragement and assistance:

Gordon F. Aiavao
Oscar Brito
Alicia Buffa
Thomas Collins
BJ Corbitt
Sherman Hayes
Scott Hooker
Linda Hoover
Madaline Leonick
Elizabeth Lewis
Regina Mayorga
Mary Mitchell
Christy Rabe
Erika Slivka
Doug Vaughn

CPSIA information can be obtained at www.ICGtesting.com
Printed in the USA
BVOW07s1859260913

332246BV00001B/22/P